Samri Baldwin

**Secrets Of Mahatma Land Explained**

Samri Baldwin

**Secrets Of Mahatma Land Explained**

ISBN/EAN: 9783742862679

Manufactured in Europe, USA, Canada, Australia, Japa

Cover: Foto ©Andreas Hilbeck / pixelio.de

Manufactured and distributed by brebook publishing software
(www.brebook.com)

Samri Baldwin

**Secrets Of Mahatma Land Explained**

## SAMRI S. & MRS. KITTIE

# BALDWIN

# THE WHITE MAHATMAS,

### AND THEIR COMPANY OF

# HIGH CLASS ENTERTAINERS.

NOW ON THEIR FIFTH TOUR AROUND THE WORLD WITH THE QUEEREST, QUAINTEST, MOST BEWILDERING AND FASCINATING ENTER-
TAINMENT EVER PRESENTED TO THE PUBLIC.

MORE THAN FIVE THOUSAND EMINENT CLERGYMEN HAVE WRITTEN TO
PROFESSOR BALDWIN PRAISING HIS ENTERTAIMENT AS BEING
CLEAN, PURE, HIGH CLASS AND EXTREMELY
ATTRACTIVE IN EVERY PARTICULAR.

Permanent address in England:

**Prof. S. S. Baldwin,**
c/o Williams & Co.
8 School Lane,
Liverpool,
England.

Permanent American Address:

**Prof. S. S. Baldwin,**
Calhoun Printing Co.
Hartford,
Conn, U. S. A.

Letters sent to either of the above addresses will always reach Prof. Baldwin.
Always enclose a stamped and addressed envelope for reply.

Prof. SAMRI S. BALDWIN.

## PREFACE TO THE SECOND EDITION.

### SPECIAL EXPLANATION.

The first edition (comprising ten thousand copies) of this work was printed in Australia. The sale was so unexpectedly great that it was sold out within a few months. Unfortunately not a single copy was left and this edition was very hurriedly rewritten from memory. With the present edition there were many accidents, and it is full of mistakes and typographical errors, not really the fault of the printer but due to extreme haste and imperfect proofreading on my part (caused by illness and great press of other business).

When this edition was contemplated it was largely advertised and many orders were taken, but a fire at first and other accidents later on caused an unavoidable delay in its issue.

---

---

PRESS OF T. J. DYSON & SON,
938, 960 and 962 Washington Street,
Brooklyn, N. Y.

# PREFACE.

By DOCTOR FRANK BALDWIN.

PROF. Samri S. Baldwin, known through the East as " The White Mahatma ;" a title which he has since adopted for exhibition purposes, was born in Cincinnati, Ohio.

At an early age he displayed a decided penchant for dabbling in the mysterious. One of the first thrashings, but by no means the only one he ever received, was for cutting two holes in the family dining table, so that a small youngster hidden underneath could change an egg into a potato.

After considerable practice he was able to accomplish this to his own satisfaction. The egg was placed at one end of the table, the potato at the other, each being covered with a tea cup, *presto change!* and with a flourish of his wand the cups were removed and behold the egg and potato had changed places.

At this stage the family and neighbors were called in to witness the remarkable transformation. But alas for the uncertainty of human affairs. When the cups were lifted and everybody should have been transfixed with amazement, a cruel and prosaic mother, who was herself a bit of a sleight-of-hand performer, discovered that her dining table was ruined. The small boy underneath the table was fished out with the crooked end of an umbrella and ignominiously thrown into the street ; while S. S. was painfully made aware of the truth of the Scriptural saying : that " To spare the rod spoils the child," and for some days thereafter he took his meals in comfort off the mantel-piece, while his mother consoled him with other adages, such as "A thrashing in time saves nine." etc., etc.

As he became older all his spare spending money was expended in buying the " Magician's Own Book," " The Boy's Book of Magic," etc. In 1864, he commenced making experiments in White Magic. Shortly afterwards he witnessed the perform-ances of the far-famed Davenport Brothers, and became entirely fascinated with the weird, and at the time, to him, inexplicable doings. He followed the Davenport Brothers from town to town and place to place, but soon became convinced that all of their work was but very dextrous and delicate deception.

He then took up the subject of Spiritualism and occult phenomena in general, and all his evenings were occupied in attending spiritual seances.

After a few years investigation he became absolutely skeptical as to anything spiritual, and became certain that most if not all of the so called spiritual and supernatural manifestations were produced either by conscious or unconscious deception, or caused by natural, though not well understood laws.

He commenced a series of entertainments in which he first duplicated and then explained the manifestations of the fraudulent mediums. And for a long time offered a reward of five hundred dollars for any manifestation which he could not show was produced by human agency, if he was first permitted to witness it twice.

Having a natural gift for thaumaturgy, he added to his entertainment several remarkable deceptions of his own, and from the very start created a furore, crowding the largest théatres, and causing immense excitement, by the weird and startling results produced without any apparatus of any sort.

Almost every clergyman of any note visited the entertainment and in many places the *performances were spoken of from the pulpits as being a great benefit to the public at large.* Thousands of eminent public individuals sent Professor Baldwin most complimentary letters and testimonials testifying to the good he was doing.

In the very zenith of his success his health broke down and he was forced to rest. He went to India and the East and spent many months in investigating the Rosocrucian mysteries and feats of the Thibetian Mahatmas.

Again he commenced his entertainments, and all over the Orient created a most profound sensation. His hypnotic and clairvoyant trance experiments especially causing much discussion. He visited Great Britain, and for seven months drew enormous audiences, but once more breaking down was compelled to seek warmer climates. He has visited nearly all the capitals of Europe, Northern Africa, Turkey in Asia, Arabia and Egypt, South Africa, Bechuana Land, Natal, Zulu Land, Delagoa Bay, Zanzibar, and the African East Coast, Mauritius, Ceylon, India, Burma, Siam, China, Japan, Java, Borneo, and Sumatra, all parts of Australia, Tasmania, New Zealand, Fiji Islands, New Caledonia, Samoa, Honolulu and the Hawaiian Islands, British Columbia, Canada, all parts of the United States, Mexico, Central America and Cuba, and portions of South America. Everywhere the largest theatres and halls have been crowded to suffocation.

Professor Baldwin does not believe in the supernatural or occult. In his opinion the manifestations of the mediums ; the sorcery of the Yogii and the mysticism of the Mahatmas are wonderful only because not generally understood. In his Oriental entertainments Professor Baldwin added to the conjuration of the Indian Ojha Brahmins bewildering artifices of his own, and, although India and the East are the very birthplace of occult mysteries, yet Professor Baldwin's entertainment was so marvellous in its weird fascination that Fakeers and Phongyii, Brahmins and Ascetics, Laamas and Gooroos, in their amazement christened Professor Baldwin "The mighty monarch of the Mahatmas."

" His talk is redolent of the humor characteristic of Mark Twain and Artemus Ward, and keeps his audience in a simmer of merriment, while his peculiar performance adds a flavor of deep mystery to the proceedings."

# INDEX.

INDEX—Continued.

## LIST OF ILLUSTRATIONS.

# CHAPTER I.

## THE ORIENTAL DEFINITION OF A MAHATMA.

WHAT PEOPLE THINK A MAHATMA IS. WHAT A MAHATMA REALLY IS. HOW I RECEIVED THE TITLE, "WHITE MAHATMA." TRAVELERS' YARNS. ILLUSIONARY FAKEERS. INDIAN SLEIGHT OF HAND. THE WITCH OF ENDOR. MY FIRST INDIAN EXPERIENCE. HOW I BECAME DISGUSTED.

IT is a common thing nowadays to talk about Mahatmas, but not one person in a thousand, even among the educated men and women of the day, who use the word "Mahatma" so fluently and flippantly, has the slightest idea of what a Mahatma is.

According to the Eastern idea, spiritually speaking, a Mahatma is simply one who has so purified his "Mahat" or spiritual mind or inner nature, that his higher ego is enabled to act directly upon his lower or brain mind. When this occurs he becomes a Mahatma, or "great soul." This is the literal definition of Mahatma. The popular or common idea of a Mahatma is, one who is capable of performing strange mysteries and producing remarkable and semi-miraculous demonstrations by some occult or unknown agency.

Referring, however, to the spiritual idea of the Mahatma, a modern writer to an English paper says : "In order, therefore, to see a Mahatma and to recognize him as such, it is necessary to contact him upon his own spiritual plane. Elevate your consciousness to the Mahatmic plane, and you will see not *a* Mahatma, but many. It is true that a Mahatma may reveal himself to some person or persons on the 'outer' plane—for purposes of his own, but in such a case the evidence of his Mahatmaship rests in the consciousness of the person or persons who see or contact him, not in the display of any abnormal powers. And deception—unconscious or conscious—is easy. And we may be perfectly sure that no Mahatma will appear for the sake of proving his existence. He works for other ends and wider issues. Mahatma is a name for an internal and spiritual condition and does not depend in any way upon outside circumstances, conditions or powers. For anything you know to the contrary, the ragged being who sweeps the streets in front of your house or office may be a Mahatma, or be on the high road to Mahatmaship. It has been said that you might live in the same house with a Mahatma all your life and never know him except as your co-dweller. Why? Because though your bodies are on the same plane your minds are on different planes. He lives in a spiritual world to which yours has not yet awakened. Meanwhile you can study the evidence (which exists in profusion) that Mahatmas are not vapors from Theosophic brains. If you cannot see a Mahatma you can read the accounts of those who have seen Mahatmas. You can compare accounts and sift circumstances. It will be a task, it is true, to do it properly, for you will have to read records going back to the earliest times, and of innumerable peoples.

PROFESSOR

# SAMRI S.

# BALDWIN

IN THE DRESS OF A

## BRAHMIN

## MAHATMA.

Mrs. KITTIE

## BALDWIN

THE

## ROSICRUCIAN

## SOMNOMIST.

If you are a Christian, perhaps you had better confine yourself to the Bible, which is full of the records of the Mahatmas, great masters, teachers, spiritual guides, adepts, whatever you like to call them."

In assuming the title of the "White Mahatma," a title which was first given me by the Indian newspapers and afterward adopted by the public at large, *I do not assume or claim the possession or use of any miraculous, occult, superhuman or supernatural powers whatever.* In fact, I do not believe in the supernatural in any sense. But as a wonder worker and mystery producer, the manifestations exhibited by my wife and myself are fully equal to any of the manifestations *given under similar conditions* by any of the Yogis or Gooroos of India or the Gompas of Thibet.

I admit that many of the stories and tales I have seen in print are decidedly of a miraculous flavor and candidly confess that I cannot explain them as thus told.

Many of the traveler's stories are similar to those of the little boy at a birthday party, who pointed at a little girl and said : " This little girl is my own blood sister, yet her father is not my father, and her mother is not my mother." Every one puzzled himself to guess how this could be. The solution finally was that the little boy had lied. So, in many of the travelers yarns, a very little grain of fact is seized upon and woven and distorted into a tissue of exaggeration and fiction marvelous to read, but perhaps without the slightest modicum of real truth.

It must be remembered that millions of people who have lived in India all their lives have never seen the manifestations claimed to be produced by the Yogis. The majority of Indian residents set the whole thing down as mere bosh and contemptuously ridicule the stories they read as being the grossest exaggeration or the most positive falsehoods.

My own experience has been, that laying aside the exaggerations of travelers and even the deliberate fabrications of writers wishing to make their books sell, or to produce newspaper or magazine articles palatable to the desire of the public for something beyond the ordinary ken, that there are a very few individuals in India who are capable of causing the spectators who are in their immediate proximity to see or to *imagine* they see most remarkable and astounding occurrences. These favored individuals, however, are very few and are rarely met with even by Indian residents.

The ordinary illusionary fakeer is quite common, and the production of the Mango tree, the Basket illusion and other work of that character can be witnessed in almost every Indian town with as much frequency as street bands or hand organs can be heard in other countries.

These illusionary fakeers, however, do not produce anything like the class of work which is said to be produced by the Yogis, and it is the illusionary work which is mostly witnessed by globe-trotters, to whom it seems extremely marvelous; but to professionals, who understand the principle of the various deceptions, much of their work seems very poor. Most of these fakeers, however, are, in the strict sense of the word, marvelous *sleight of hand* performers. Their sleight and dexterity in minor ledgerdemain is something beautiful to see. None of it, however, is in any sense more dextrous than the three-card manipulations of the ordinary "monte" men, or the work of the "thimble rigger," so often to be seen on English race courses.

In this volume, which I term "The Secrets of Mahatma Land Exposed," I take the broad definition of a Mahatma to be a mystery worker and producer of weird, strange and bewildering manifestations; in fact, the Sorcerers or Magii of the various countries in which I have traveled.

Any American spiritual medium, according to the testimony of thousands who have claimed to have witnessed materializations and other phenomena of that character, is just as much deserving of the title of Mahatma as any of the Oriental mystery workers.

In all sections of the world, and ever since the creation, there have been people credited with having supernatural powers. We read in the Bible that people of this class had become so common in the days of Saul (and had perhaps deceived

THE YOGII AT THE NAG-PUNCHMI, OR THE FESTIVAL OF THE SERPENTS, BOMBAY.

the public with the same facility that their modern confreres have done) that Saul was forced to issue an edict casting them out of the land. But being himself infected by the popular belief in their miraculous powers, he decided to consult the Witch of Eudor, and, if we are to believe all we read about her, she undoubtedly got rather the better of her kingly applicant and humbugged him to her heart's content.

In Africa, the Obi man, Witch doctor and Rainmaker hold the same position in the estimation of the people. The North American Indian has his Medicine man; Voodooism still has hold of the West India negro and Shamonism controls even the fur-clad Esquimaux.

It is almost useless to contend against a belief which seems engrafted in the entire population of the world.

Superstition dies hard, and perhaps as long as the world lasts people will believe (because they wish to) that certain favored individuals are possessed of occult and superhuman powers.

Personally, I do not believe in the occult or superhuman. Every manifestation I have yet seen seems to me to be based upon nature's immutable and unchangeable laws. The mere fact of our not understanding these laws does not make occurrences by their agency supernatural. On the contrary, it shows ignorance and should incite to serious study and sensible investigation.

When I first went to India, I had heard and read so much about the marvels to be seen there that I was in a good condition to be deceived. I *wanted* to see something marvelous and hoped and felt sure that I would see something that I could not understand or comprehend. Fortunately for me, however, my first experience was with some of the wandering fakeers. A friend of mine who had resided in India some few months previous to my arrival was much impressed with some of the tricks he had seen on the street, and was impressed by them because they were done in the open. His theory about modern Caucasian magicians was that all of their mysteries were caused by concealed stage trap-doors, and that the average illusionist was capable of producing from his coat sleeve anything from a bird cage to a hippopotamus.

But he was decidedly fascinated by the delicate sleight of hand of the fakeers. He, like myself, had read a lot, and wished to believe in the marvels of the East. But, unlike myself, he was not acquainted with the tricks and deceptions of 'hanky panky', illusionists. Therefore, when he first saw the Basket trick and the growth of the Mango tree, he at once decided that some occult force must be at work.

Knowing, however, my skeptical disposition regarding anything supernatural, he was quite anxious to have me see the identical performances which had so puzzled him and felt quite sure I would at once be converted to a belief in occult forces when I saw the doings of a particular fakeer and his assistants.

I was, however, much disappointed. The first time I saw their performances many of the tricks seemed ridiculously simple, and I stared in perfect wonderment at the mystified appearance of my friends and some European lookers on who seemed thoroughly bewildered by what they saw.

My friend turned on me triumphantly at the conclusion of the Basket trick and said: "There! can you see any possible explanation?"

I said: "Is it *possible* you cannot see how simple it is? It seems to me every one must see through it."

His reply was: "Is it *possible* you really see through it and can honestly explain it?"

"To me it seems very trumpery" was my answer. "But perhaps the man is not a first-class performer."

An old Indian resident standing near, assured me that he had seen many of the fakeers and that the man before us was a very fair sample of his kind. The thermometer of my faith in Indian miracles fell to zero, and though afterward I saw many fakeers and yogis and saw much that was interesting and even puzzling, I never saw any one thing done that could give me any faith in the reality of occultism.

A SAVAGE ILLUSIONIST'S ASSISTANT.

HINDU SNAKE CHARMERS AND FAKEERS.

## CHAPTER II.

### MY DEFINITION OF A MAHATMA.

SECRETS OF MAHATMA LAND EXPLAINED. THE DAVENPORT BROTHERS AND PROFESSOR
FAY. CHARLES FOSTER, THE MEDIUM. MY SEANCES. FOSTER'S BLOOD WRIT-
ING EXPLAINED. FIVE DOLLARS OF SPIRITUAL TRICKERY LEARNED FOR FIFTY
CENTS. DOCTORS SLADE AND MANSFIELD. ANNA STEWART AND MRS. SAWYER.
KNAVES VS. FOOLS. CONFESSIONS OF MEDIUMS.

A Mahatma is then, to be brief, merely a mystery-worker, and this volume,
"*Secrets of Mahatma Land Exposed*," is a brief itinerary of my travels in various
parts of the world in search of mysteries *and the secret of their production*. In addition to my own accounts it will contain copious quotations from the writings of
others, describing this class of people and their work and deceptions of all sorts, no
matter in what section of the world they are to be found.

I believe I have a natural talent in this particular line. I think I may say this
without egotism, for few people succeed largely in any line of work without having
some aptitude for it, and in the investigation and detection of the modus operandi of
mysteries, it is so evidently to the interest of the miracle-mongers to keep their
secrets to themselves, that unless one has a special capability and liking for this
branch of work he will learn very little.

Years ago, so long ago in fact that I dread to look back at it, as it reminds me
how fast the time has flown, I witnessed a performance by the then world-famed
Davenport Brothers and Professor Fay. I was simply fascinated by it. It seemed
to me so strange and unreal that I can quite well forgive myself for the belief which
I at first had that the queer, weird manifestations were produced by an agency supernatural.

For several nights I sat in the front row before I dared go upon the stage. Then
my natural curiosity got the better of me, I suppose upon the principle that "famil-
iarity breeds contempt." I began to turn over in my mind if it were not possible to
produce these same results by some delicate chicanery. True, it seemed impossible.
But for that matter so did the tricks of the illusionists I had witnessed, and I determined, if it could be done, to solve the mystery. I procured a walking-stick which
I divided carefully into inches, so as to make a measuring rod out of it. During the
intermission when the audience were allowed to inspect the cabinet and the ropes I
went upon the stage, and night after night carefully measured the length, breadth
and depth of the cabinet, took notes of the length of the ropes, their construction,
etc., and afterward made experiments at home with my friends. Here was where my
natural aptitude for this work was of great benefit to me. I found that I could produce
the same work under exactly the same conditions, and that I could do it by trickery.
My work seemed just as marvelous to my friends and companions as the work of
the Davenports had seemed to me. I then coaxed a number of friends to visit the
Davenports' performance to see if there was any comparable difference between their
work and mine. My work was voted equally as mysterious as theirs, and the conditions I gave for examination and investigation were rather better. I then

SELF LACERATION BY THE YOGII.

commenced to add little tricks of my own, and in a very short time my performances were not only equal to those of the Davenport Brothers but were infinitely superior. About that time Charles Foster, the medium, came along and he interested me more than the Davenports did. I became so infatuated with his work that I had at different times over thirty sittings with this gentleman at $5 each. It did not take the entire thirty sittings to convince me that I was being humbugged much of the time. That, I became sure of after some half dozen seances. But I attended the remaining number of times with a view of getting at the secret of his work. The conclusion I finally arrived at, and which I still hold in regard to this gentleman's manifestations, was that he had considerable natural clairvoyant, telepathic or mindreading powers. I also found that he could not always exercise this faculty, and in cases where he could not get the results normally, he deceived his sitters by delicate sleight of hand.

The famous "blood writing" which Foster was the first medium to introduce, I found could very readily be duplicated, but it is an experiment which can not be given by every one.

I will explain it in order that the reader may understand how bewildering it was. Foster, after first telling his visitor some startling facts about various dead friends and relations, would suddenly show the palm of his hand, or bare his arm to the elbow, and show the sitter that it contained no marks or writing of any sort. He would then place his arm under the table and ask "the spirit" to write his or her name on the arm. The arm was then rubbed briskly with the hand, the fingers of the hand generally being slightly moistened, when there would be a pale, pink writing, slightly in relief, as if a thread or cord was underneath the flesh. The lines of the writing would sometimes be sufficiently raised so as to be perceptible to the touch as well as to sight. After a few moments the writing would disappear. Of course, it was claimed and generally supposed by the sitters that this writing was produced by some supernatural agency.

As a matter of fact the bit of deception was very simple, and was produced in the following manner.

Mr. Foster, either by his natural clairvoyant power or by a sleight of hand process, which at present I have not space to explain, first obtained the name of the dead relation or individual whom the visitor wished to communicate with. Then, taking an ordinary match, or small piece of wood sharpened to a point, the point being rounded and somewhat blunt, yet fairly fine. While walking up and down the room, but generally while lighting his cigar, for he usually smoked most of the time during the seance, he would write upon the arm or hand exactly as if he was writing with a lead pencil, only using the point of the match, and pressing very hard. At first for a moment or two the writing is not at all legible, nor will it show. The arm is then placed under the table for a few seconds, ostensibly to give the spirits a chance to write. Then when withdrawn from underneath the table, if the fingers are dampened and rubbed rapidly and firmly a number of times over the place where the writing was made, a bright pink letter will develop. This cannot be produced by everybody. It requires a skin of peculiar quality, but perhaps six or seven people out of every ten can produce the experiment without the slightest trouble.

After seeing Foster I visited almost every medium of note in the United States, Slade, Mansfield, Cutler, Anna Stewart, Mrs. Sawyer, and hundreds of others that I cannot now mention. The more I investigated the more I became convinced that, outside of a few manifestations or exhibitions in telepathic or mind-reading force, that the work of all the so-called spiritualistic mediums was produced absolutely and entirely by trickery. I refer now to physical manifestations. such as table rapping, table lifting, levitation of bodies, precipitation, materialization and work of that character.

I have attended at least two thousand spiritual seances, and I am more convinced

CAMBODIAN RAIN MAKER.

now even than I was in my earlier days, that under no circumstances do disembodied spirits return to this world to produce manifestations of any character.

I believe that in a few cases where the mental manifestations are exhibited that they are produced without intentional deception on the part of the medium, especially where the medium is a private individual, giving manifestations without pay or reward. But even then, in many cases the physical manifestations (and even the so-called mental work) are quite often produced knowingly and wilfully by the medium. But, it is often objected, why should an individual who gets no gain or profit out of the matter stoop to deceive friends and acquaintances. The reason is very simple. Nine people out of every ten would rather be slightly knavish than be regarded as fools.

Usually the private mediums who play tricks of this character in their sittings, in the first place have an earnest belief in spiritualism. They have in many cases been told by professional mediums that they possess clairvoyant or mediumistic power, and are very often much flattered to think that they have some abnormal quality which the average individual has not. It is quite a common thing for a medium to say to a visitor: "You have remarkable mediumistic powers, if you would only develop them. You should have a number of developing sittings." The embryo medium at once commences what he or she believes to be a course of development. Private circles are formed, consisting of perhaps half a dozen individuals.

Occasionally the servant or the governess is included, sons or daughters of the family, visitors, etc.

Now, in a circle of this kind, composed of a half dozen persons, it is almost a certainty that there will be some roguish individual, who, without any idea of harm, quietly has a little fun on his or her own account at the expense of the circle. It is quite a tedious matter to sit at a table from half an hour to an hour at a time waiting for the spirits to make some manifestations. The spirits do not manifest, and after one or two sittings of this kind the roguish individual concludes to "help the spirits."

There are a dozen ways in which little raps can be produced. The table is slightly and quietly tilted to one side. The earnest inquirers in the circle are, of course, quite honest in the matter, and the family trickster, very often a demure young lady, or even an old one for that matter, unhesitatingly affirms that they are quite passive and that it is most wonderful how the manifestations occur. The would-be medium of course gets the credit of developing rapidly. By and by the roguish member of the circle gets tired of the mummery and when the circle is made up usually finds some excuse to be absent. Or, if forced to be one of the number, gets what little amusement he can by keeping up the manifestations. Should the direct factor of the manifestations, however, be absent, after a few sittings the members of the circle become tired. The medium, who is at first honestly intent on developing the powers he imagines he possesses and having his hopes excited, is very often led to deliberately simulate the manifestations by a trick sooner than not be thought a medium, or to be deemed a fool by the other members of the circle.

I have known dozens of cases where the mediums have confessed to me that after having had a number of developing sittings, and finding that the spirits would not come, that "just for a bit of fun," they themselves produced the demonstrations.

Again, in the case of children and very young ladies and gentlemen, very often they are flattered and pleased by the amount of attention and curiosity they excite. It gives them a certain little local notoriety. They are looked upon and pointed out as being rather above the ordinary run of individuals. In fact, it makes them quite a little lion in their local circle. They do not see any particular harm in thus affecting powers they do not possess. Many times I have had people say to me: "There is my daughter, who gets the most wonderful manifestations. She does not do it for money, but only with our own family and a few friends. How do you account for her manifestations?" Upon making the acquaintance of the daughter and gaining her confidence, and perhaps for a time or two at her seances assisting her quietly, she has confessed to me that her parents have imagined her a great medium. and it seemed to please them so much that she thought it was rather amusing and harmless to keep them so interested in it.

It is a well-known fact that dozens of people will do things for a matter of pride or reputation, or to make themselves prominent, that they would not do for money. The desire and craving for notoriety are so strong in some people that they would almost commit murder to be thought out of the commonplace.

## CHAPTER. III.

## MY TRAVELS CONTINUED.

I GO TO AUSTRALIA, INDIA AND CEYLON. A FAKEER ON FIRE. NAKED NATIVES AND STARTLED SORCERERS. AN ILLUSIONIST ILLUMINATED. BOMBAY RAWM SAMMY FRIGHTENED. HOW I DID IT. LIQUID LIGHTNING. CONCENTRATED HADES.

To resume my travels, however. After becoming thoroughly expert and *au fait* in the work of the mediums, I commenced entertainments duplicating and thoroughly exposing and explaining the secret of their work. And I may say right here, that I have never yet seen any manifestation of any sort given by any spiritual medium which *I was not quite sure was produced solely and purely by human and natural agencies.*

I commenced a Western tour at Nashville, Tennessee. From there went to Cincinnati, Indianapolis, St. Louis, Chicago, Detroit, Cleveland, Pittsburg, Kansas City and the larger cities and towns in the West and Southwest. Thence to the Pacific Coast. In all this section I created an absolute sensation. In most places the largest theatres were packed to suffocation. Toronto, Montreal, Quebec and Halifax were next. Then Boston, Fall River, Providence and the larger Eastern cities. The late Dr. Geo. M. Beard, an eminent physician in New York city, arranged with me to come to Brooklyn and give two entertainments at the Y. M. C. A. Hall. Under his auspices I also delivered several lectures and expositions at Cooper Institute in New York city.

All at once my health began to fail, and after consultation with physicians, I decided upon a long sea trip and sailed for Australia.

The voyage was of immense benefit to me, and on reaching Australia my entertainments created a positive furore.

In Sydney for fifteen weeks a large hall, seating nearly two thousand people, was always crowded, and in Melbourne for the same length of time at St. George's Hall people were nightly turned away.

I spent nearly fifteen months in Australia and returned to America for a few months, then went to England. Here, for five months, I had very large audiences, but my health again gave way and I sailed for South Africa, putting in some eight months in that country.

From Africa I went to Ceylon; from Ceylon to Madras and Calcutta, and then put in some eight months in India. Most of the time being in the northeast provinces.

In Bombay I appeared before Sir James Ferguson, the Governor. I also appeared before the Governor at Madras and the Viceroy, Lord Ripon, in Calcutta.

In Ceylon I witnessed my first exhibition of traveling Indian Fakeers. In Bombay, too, there were so many of them they became almost a nuisance.

One could hardly step on the street or gaze an instant into the bazaar windows, when some Fakeer would suddenly squat in front of you and produce the implements of his trade. In one case I was invited to dine with one of the local magnates and quite a large party had assembled. For my gratification a number of the

highest class Fakeers had been especially engaged to produce their most marvelous work before me. Although it was very dextrous and skillful, I was really
much disappointed, as it did not come up to the yarns I had read, so I sprang a little surprise upon them which not only thoroughly startled and frightened the Fakeers
and native on-lookers, but completely bewildered the European guests as well.

As the Fakeers were about to conclude their performance I asked permission of
my host to show them a sample of my skill. I instructed the interpreter to say to
the Fakeers in the grandiloquent manner of the East, that I was much disappointed with so paltry a performance. That I personally was the King and Emperor
of all magicians, and knowing, as he did, that he was to appear before a *Bellatee*
(or English) professional he should have provided, if he was able, far more wonderful tricks. That in showing us such rubbish he had insulted the gentleman who had
employed him and the guests as well, and that I intended by my magical powers
to punish him for his impudence.

I informed him that I should simply wave my hand a half dozen times and cause
fire to spring from the air and consume him and his companions unless he at once
showed us something more marvelous.

He informed me with a sneer that he had already shown me the best work to
be seen in the East, and that he was not in the least afraid of what I could do to

A FIJI SORCERER.

him. That as a worker of magic he thoroughly understood all the processes, and
I was simply trying to frighten him without being able to carry out my threats,
and rather curtly hinted that I was talking too much.

I immediately stepped to within four or five feet of him and commenced
waving my hands in the air. Then suddenly clapping them together I commanded
that he and his assistants be struck with lightning. Suddenly, to his inexplicable
horror, the kummerband and breechclout, which are pretty well all the clothes these
fellows wear, burst into a blaze, and he and his assistants were enveloped in flames.
They immediately rushed for the gate of the "compound," as the inclosure or yard
surrounding the building is called, frantically tearing their clothing off as they went,
and by the time they reached the street they were nude as when they came into
the world. There they stood, half dazed, more frightened than hurt, staring at

each other, rubbing their arms and bodies where they had been uncomfortably hot, and wondering how it had all happened. The English guests and spectators of the affair were screaming with laughter. My host, who had lived in India the greater part of his life, and was thoroughly acquainted with all of their remarkable illusions, declared that my experiment was far more wonderful than anything he had ever seen.

The solution of the mystery was very simple, although I did not then acquaint any one with the secret. I had prepared a chemical preparation, which, when poured upon paper, wood or inflammable material of any kind, shortly becomes perfectly invisible and cannot be detected by the sharpest observer. In a time varying from one to three minutes (depending upon the temperature and method of manufacture) this chemical spontaneously ignites and the article upon which it may have been poured instantly burns like tinder.

My own Indian servant, who had been carefully drilled by me, had a small homeopathic vial with a glass stopper, carried in a wet rag in his hand, and by mingling with the other Indian servants and household attendants who crowded around the Fakeer and his assistants, was enabled at a signal from me. to place a few drops of this preparation, unknown to the magicians, upon the flimsy cotton garments which were wrapped around them. I timed my talk so as to fit in when I knew the stuff would ignite. And the spectacle of three or four men bursting into a blaze at my bidding, while I was some yards distant, was enough to terrify the most cynical Fakeer that Indian soil ever produced.

This same trick was often given by me in various ways, mostly at private assemblages, as it was too dangerous to use often at public entertainments, though I occasionally used it even then and it always caused the greatest surprise and consternation.

In the case above mentioned the clothing of the Hindoos was replaced for a few rupees and the present of another five or ten rupees thoroughly healed their wounded feelings and sent them away delighted to spread all over the country a report of my great power.

# CHAPTER IV.

## BURMA AND KING THEBAW.

I visited Burma next. At Rangoon our entertainments were so very successful that a merchant there fancied we would surely do well at Mandalay. He was under the impression that we could appear before King Thebaw and the nobles of the Burmese capital and create an enormous sensation. So after much dickering as to terms, as I myself was very anxious to visit northern Burma, it was finally arranged that we were to receive three thousand rupees per week and the expenses of my wife, my assistants and myself. We had a very pleasant but rather tedious trip to Mandalay. We expected, as I stated, to create quite a surprise. The surprise certainly was there, but it was we who were surprised and not King Thebaw and his royal courtiers.

We had not very much trouble to get an audience with the King, and were commanded to give our entertainment at the Royal Silver Palace, a beautiful building since destroyed by fire. It was evident from the first that the King was in a state of beastly intoxication, or stupidity, caused perhaps by bhang or opium, for he appeared almost maudlin. He, however, seemed very much impressed with the first two or three illusions which I presented. All of a sudden a thought seemed to strike him, and. stopping the performance he spoke to the interpreter and said: "Where are the presents these people have brought me? Have they brought no diamonds or jewels?" The interpreter with much fear and trepidation explained that we were only poor "show people," whose sole wish was to give an entertainment which would please His Royal Highness. That we had not brought diamonds or jewelry as presents. For anything which we could give would be so trumpery in comparison to the beautiful jewels he already possessed that they would appear insignificant. This explanation instead of pacifying the irate monarch only seemed to make him all the more indignant. In a few gruff words he commanded that we immediately leave the palace and get out of Mandalay as soon as possible, as he considered that he was insulted by not being given valuable presents by people who were enjoying the benefit of his royal patronage and the protection of his laws.

We immediately left Mandalay. Glad to get away with our lives. It was well that we did so, for a few days afterward occurred the terrible massacre at the royal palace, where the king's wife caused some sixty or seventy of her royal relations, nobles and others, whom she disliked and feared, to be quietly murdered. They were all invited to a grand banquet, and that night by her orders were slaughtered in cold blood. This horrible deed and many others of a like nature was the prelude of the Burmese war, which was followed by the abdication and flight of King Thebaw and the occupation of the entire country by the British.

It may not be generally known that the Burmese monarchs, in order to mate only with those of royal blood, always marry within their own family. King Thebaw himself married *seven of his own sisters*, and the favorite one of these seven wives, by her jealousy, caused the murder of so many of the royal relations.

I then went to Penang, Singapore, Bangkok, Siam, Hong Kong, Shanghai, Amoy and Foochow.

During one of my trips, myself and party witnessed the execution by decapitation of sixteen pirates at Koolong, opposite Hong Kong. They were executed by order of the Chinese authorities.

With hands and feet bound they knelt in a row along the beach, and the executioner, with a huge sword, cut off their heads. He was not more than two or three minutes killing the entire sixteen. The heads were neatly chopped off, never

AN ADVENTURE IN BURMA.

taking more than one blow of the heavy sword, and occasionally they flew to a distance of four or five feet from the body. Before the execution commenced the friends of the criminals were allowed to give them opium to blunt their senses. As they were kneeling on the ground, one man, the eighth or ninth in the row, looking along to the right, seemed much interested by the manner in which the executioner took off the heads of the seven or eight before his own turn came. As the second head went off he was highly amused, and a broad grin overspread his face. As the third and fourth heads fell to the dextrous stroke of the executioner, the living culprit fairly roared with merriment, stooping over and bowing his own head just as his turn came, and as his head fell his features were still relaxed with laughter.

' Another pirate, number eleven in the row, wished to be quite defiant, and instead of stooping over and holding his head in a position to receive a fair blow of the sword, he defiantly held his head and body perfectly upright, so that the executioner could not well strike him. The Mandarin who had charge of the affair directed the executioner to draw the sword slowly across the back of the man's neck, and thus cut a deep gash, so the man would bleed profusely and become weakened. This was done. The executioner then passed on and chopped off the heads of the remaining five pirates. Upon returning to number eleven, who was still obstinate, and struggling his best to retain an upright position, the executioner became annoyed, and placing his foot between the man's shoulder blades, pushed him sharply forward, striking at him as he fell. The head was taken off clean and smooth, the force of the blow causing it to fly several yards.

It was a most ghastly sight, but was witnessed by quite a number of Europeans and several thousand Chinese. There has certainly been much less piracy in that neighborhood since.

From Shanghai we visited Pekin, where we appeared before the young Emperor, the dowager Empress and the Imperial court. Returning to Shanghai we went to Japan. While in Japan I went into the interior of the country, spending some months there. The mode of transportation then being mostly by *jin-ricsha* (a little two-wheeled buggy, something resembling a large baby carriage), or by Sedan chair, carried by two or four coolies.

Along the roadside, in a beautiful mountain gorge, near a little village, I was suddenly transfixed with horror at beholding the body of a malefactor who had been crucified. He was fastened by the feet and hands to a rude cross-like structure. His head had been partially severed from the body with a stroke of a sword, and was hanging to one side, while two other cuts of the sword had disemboweled him.

' In Yokohama I had great success, so much so that I was invited to Tokio, and as a most unusual favor to me I was asked to give my entertainment before the Mikado, who presented me with a very large number of valuable presents.

From Yokohama I returned to Hong Kong, Singapore, and thence into Java and Borneo. I visited many places where I could not give entertainments, solely with the view of studying the customs and manners of the people.

At Sarawak we went some distance up in the country, running considerable risk. But my reputation as a miracle-worker had preceded me, and I was generally received with courtesy and kindness. We occasionally gave entertainments before the native Princes. Of course, the programme was not the same as we gave to English-speaking audiences, for, as all talking was done through an interpreter, I had to arrange a programme that could be comprehended by the audiences without much speaking on my part.

The spontaneous ignition trick, which I have previously mentioned, always caused the most profound astonishment, in some cases mingled with deep awe and fright. It was rarely ever given as a regular item in the entertainment. I usually kept it to spring as a sudden surprise in places where the people were not looking for an exhibition of my powers.

¶We gave an entertainment one afternoon before a native audience composed almost entirely of the family and immediate attendants of one of the old head-hunting Dyak chiefs. This old chap in his time had, perhaps, been a cannibal, but modern rifles and European troops had for some time pretty well stopped his head-hunting expeditions. He still retained many evidences of his prowess in previous days. We were received in a large structure which was practically only a roof without inclosed ends or sides. Whenever it was necessary to have protection from the elements, light mats of bamboo or platted grasses were hung upon high posts erected at little distances apart. All around this shed, on top of these posts, were the grinning and ghastly skulls which, from time to time, had been removed by himself from the shoulders of the aged king's enemies in battle. He was much delighted with my entertainment, and his daughter, a savage beauty about fourteen or fifteen, at which age in that country native women appear at their best, was equally pleased, and through an interpreter complimented my wife and I very highly. In order to say something very pleasant, I remarked that I was surprised at the number of beautiful women I had seen in the Island, and ended by paying a high compliment to the personal appearance of the young lady in question,

INDIAN EGG DANCE.

saying, that if ever I married again, I should be highly delighted to find one so beautiful and accomplished as she, and that I would like very much to live in her village the rest of my natural life. The young lady at first seemed rather perplexed, but soon a look of complacency came over her features. She held quite a little animated conversation with her father and other members of the court, and I could tell by .the look on the face of the interpreter, and the few words which he muttered to me under his breath, that I was the subject of the conversation.

Presently a look of astonishment, mingled with horror, came over the face of my interpreter, and he managed to make me understand in his half-broken English that my compliment had been taken earnestly, and I probably had gotten myself into a serious scrape. I was informed that my flattery had been taken as a declaration of marriage and that the young lady and the old chief, her father, had decided that I was a good son-in-law to have in the family, as I could so readily strike people with lightning at a great distance and would therefore be a valuable acquisition to go with them on the warpath, and easily defeat their enemies by setting them on fire with the mere wave of my hand.

The interpreter was requested to tell me that the young lady would marry me forthwith.

Now, here was a pretty scrape for a married man. My wife was with me. If she had not been, I don't pretend to say what I might have been tempted to do. But with a jealous and infuriated English lady on one hand, and a bland and smiling Malay on the other, who would very readily stick a poisoned dagger between my ribs if I seemed to sleight her in the least, my position was not an enviable one.

I replied, however, that while I thanked the young lady very much for her very complimentary resolve to accept me as a husband, yet I was afraid she had misunderstood me, that I could not marry her *then*, as the lady who was near me was already my wife and an adept at hairpulling and other little matters of that sort.

The dusky princess informed me with a smile that it did not make the least difference. According to the custom of her people I was allowed a number of wives, six or more. She would love Mrs. Baldwin as a sister, and she fancied that Mrs. Baldwin and she between them could rule the rest of the harem without the slightest trouble.

Of course, this was one solution out of the difficulty, but I was almost in as bad a scrape as ever, for I did not want six wives. My little experience with one was enough to make me very cautious before venturing upon six at a time. I had read somewhere that "birds in their little nests agree," but I had not found any authority to assure me that six wives would agree, especially when combating between themselves for the charms of a man so handsome and fascinating as I felt sure I must be.

I was about to decline the proposition, when the interpreter explained to me that my life would. not be worth a minute's purchase unless I seemed to fall in with the plan.

I finally informed my expectant bride that I was delighted at the idea of becoming her husband, but as she was a king's daughter it was only right that the wedding festivities should be conducted in a very elaborate manner, requiring much expense. I said that I had some twenty or thirty thousand sovereigns at Singapore, only a few days' sail, but it required both my wife's presence and my own to get this money, and if she would allow one of the dignitaries of the court to proceed with me to Singapore I would return in a short time and take upon myself the marriage vows.

She seemed to think it quite reasonable that I should want my money, and gave me a detailed list of all presents that she would be glad if I would bring her. She was very affectionate with Mrs. Baldwin with whom she seemed delighted, and my wife, who regarded the thing as a great lark and who did not seem to feel my delicate position, enjoyed the whole affair quite thoroughly.

At Sarawak the British resident told me that I had made a fool of myself. In which opinion I thoroughly acquiesced. He stated that it might cause serious trouble, and the only way I could do was to arrange with the steamship agent to say they had not room for the native official who was to accompany me, but to assure him that I would return by the next boat. Upon reaching Singapore I was to send back an enormous document, formally drawn up and covered with seals and signatures of various kinds certifying that I had died. This I did. I have not been at Sarawak since, nor do I wish to go. I have no desire to be divided up among six women.

Looking at it from this distance it seems quite amusing, but while on the spot I considered myself in a very tight fix.

From Java I again proceeded to Australia, and was as successful as on my previous trip. My business was so large, in fact, that for nearly three years I remained in the country. I visited many of the up-country towns beyond the limits of railway travel. We did many hundreds of miles by coach and occasionally by ox team, having several very narrow escapes in crossing the creeks and rivers during flood time.

From Australia I went to America, intending to settle down. I found, however, that when not exhibiting and making money, it was far easier to settle down than to settle up, and again I visited England. After a few months in that country I went

INDIAN FAKEER.

through Europe to Naples, thence to Gibraltar, Morocco, Algiers, Malta, Port Said, Cairo, Alexandria, and again into India.

This time I resolved to go into Thibet. Leaving my wife in Calcutta for some months, I went by railway to Rawl Pindi, thence by *ekka* (the Indian hill cart, an awful thing to ride in), and on horseback to Srinagar. After much preparation, and accompanied by my secretary and photographer, Mr. Robert Grant, and an assistant, Mr. Frank Spencer, I essayed the difficult task of some months' exploration in Thibet. I wanted to find the Mahatmas or adepts and learn from them the secret of their marvelous work. My adventures were fortunately mostly commonplace. I ran many risks from drowning, had several severe falls while traversing the mountain passes and almost inaccessible fastnesses between Srinagar and Leh. and after an absence of some five months returned to Calcutta.

⤴ During this trip I learned much that was new to me in mesmeric and telepathic processes, but saw few physical demonstrations, even by the masters themselves, which I could not account for, either on the grounds of sheer trickery or of mesmeric or hypnotic control and influence.

The Indian Yogis certainly have acquired the secret of mesmerising or placing under mental control large numbers of people at one and the same time, and very many of the remarkable scenes and experiments which Indian travelers claim to have witnessed are but the results of mesmeric or mental hallucination.

The Thibeteans themselves are a kindly and hospitable race, but some of the customs of the country are most peculiar. The climate is so trying that only the strongest infants survive. There are far more men than women and polyandry, or a plurality of husbands, is a custom of the country. Virtue, in the sense in which it is understood in civilized countries, is neither practised nor understood. It is no uncommon thing to find one woman with four or five husbands, and one of the most embarrassing customs of the country to Europeans comes from an excess of hospitality.

Upon visiting a Thibetean who receives you as his friend or guest, his wife, or perhaps his sister or daughter, or any female member of the family, is at once brought and introduced to the visitor, with the desire that the guest should consider the female as his wife *pro tem*. Should the visitor, like myself, be troubled with excessive virtue or modesty, it places him in a decidedly awkward position. Should he refuse to accept the embraces of the lady it is considered a positive affront. No insult could be more pronounced, and I was consequently obliged to be extremely careful in accepting proffered hospitalities. To the roue who might imagine Thibet a delightful place of residence, I would here remark that the Thibetean women, while hospitable and pleasing in manner, are the reverse of charming in appearance. They are dirty and filthy in the extreme, and their company is not at all likely to be sought for or desired by any European with the slightest claims to decency or fastidiousness.

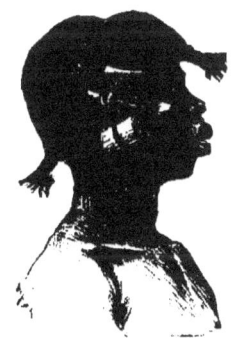

## CHAPTER V.

## A VISIT TO SRINAGAR.

**SACRED MONKEYS AND A WOMAN IN DISTRESS. FYZABAD FEMALES. I TRY TO KILL MY GRANDMOTHER AND BANG MY MOTHER-IN-LAW WITH A BRICK.**

Upon my return to Srinagar I was lucky enough to get an empty bungalo in the *Munshi Bagh*, but was unfortunately ill for some days with fever, and shortly afterwards returned to Rawl Pindi and Calcutta.

I have since then made two trips to India. On one occasion, when at Fyzabad stopping at the dak bungalo, I was much amused at the monkeys. In front of the bungalo was a large avenue of the most beautiful trees, and these trees were simply swarming with the sacred monkeys. The average Hindoo would no more think of hurting a monkey than an American or English gentleman would think of striking his mother. Monkeys are objects of love and veneration, owing to the belief of the Hindoo in the doctrine of transmigration. He believes that if he were to strike a monkey he would be injuring some relation or ancestor whose soul might inhabit the body of the impudent little beast.

At any rate, in this particular instance a Hindoo woman was walking under the trees with a bag of gram (a grain something similar to the buckwheat of America) on her shoulders.

The monkeys trooped after her for some little time, grabbing at her dress and evidently begging her to give them some of the gram. Her only remonstrance was to turn around and "shoo" at them as a Yankee woman would at her chickens. The monkeys did not mind this, but finding they could get no gram one of them suddenly ran on ahead and mounted one of the trees with a low overhanging branch. Just as the woman passed under, he let himself down with one hand and with the other gave a violent pull at her hair. The woman screamed and in her fright dropped the bag which burst open and a portion of the gram spilt over the ground. The monkeys surrounded her by the dozen, devouring it by handfuls. I was so much amused by the incident that for a moment I forgot all about the veneration of the Hindoos for monkeys and thinking to rush to the aid of a female in distress, I picked up some pieces of stone from a heap of road metal near by and caught the biggest monkey a bang under the ribs with a chunk of stone about the size of my fist. The monkey gave a scream, glared at me a second, and when I fired a second rock at him beat a retreat while I continued a fusilade upon the other members of the band. The woman herself, although evidently in great trouble over the spilling of the grain, which she was rapidly scraping together and tying up again, screamed to me, "*nay Sahib nay Sahib*," and tried her best to get me to desist.

But I was enjoying the affair. I had not had so much fun since when a boy I broke all the window glass in Joe Rhodes' house. So I pelted away delightedly, every once in a while catching some monkey a good thump in the jaw or other part of his anatomy.

Presently, to my disgust, I noticed some sixty or seventy Hindoos had collected and were muttering away, remonstrating with me in the most decided manner. The *kansamah*, or servant at the dak-bungalo, rushed out and explained to me in rather a heated manner that I was knocking the life out of the grandmothers and grand-fathers of some of the natives present, and that if I did not desist there would very probably be a riot, in which I would be torn to pieces.

As I did not like the idea of being torn to pieces I stopped. But in some fifteen or twenty minutes I was taken in charge by the military guard. The result being that I was fined some sixty rupees by an unsympathetic judge, who told me that I should mind my own business and not interfere with Hindoo customs.

In times of famine or scarcity of food these same monkeys go into the town where open bazaars, or grain and provision stores are situated, and their depredations

are quite a nuisance. They steal grain, fruit, bread, cakes and articles of that kind, much to the disgust of the shop proprietor, who can only drive them away by threats and loud scoldings, but he dare not for his life strike one of them. Sometimes a brilliant idea occurs to the bazaar-keepers to get rid of the monkeys. They dare not kill them, so large numbers are trapped, placed in sacks and carted some miles away from town by the slow bullock carts of the natives and there released. The result being that generally they arrive back in their own haunts a considerable time before the cart can return.

INDIAN NAUTCH GIRL.

# CHAPTER VI.
## I BECOME A MAHATMA.

**FEATS OF THE ZULU WITCH DOCTORS. THE MATABELE OBI MAN. WHAT HARRY KELLAR SAW. ZULU SORCERY. A LEVITATED AFRICAN. THE BURST KNOB KERRIE. THE SECRET OF THE FLOATING LOG. A MASHONA MAGICIAN.**

By means and methods which I cannot now explain, I became a member and finally a high priest of several societies devoted exclusively to the study of occult phenomena. One society had its headquarters at Benares, the other at Lucknow. And I was given an oriental title signifying "The White Mahatma."

In 1890 I returned to England and thence went into South Africa. On this trip, to give myself a little vacation, I went into the Matabele country; also into the territory of the Zulus. I gave several private entertainments in their *kraals* before the principal head men of the various tribes.

While in Africa I saw many of the medicine men, witch doctors, etc., but saw only a few manifestations of any sort. My experience in this line has been entirely different from that of my friend, Mr. Harry Kellar the eminent magician, who has been even a greater traveler than myself. A short time ago in describing some of his adventures in Zululand, Mr. Kellar said:—

But while I am speaking of this subject I may tell you of what I considered a still more wonderful feat which I witnessed in South Africa during the Zulu war. In Dunn's reservation, 200 miles north from Durban, in Natal, I saw a witch doctor levitate the form of a young Zulu by waving a tuft of grass about his head, amid surroundings calculated to impress themselves deeply upon the most prosaic imagination. It was evening, and the witch doctor, who belonged to the class described more than once by Rider Haggard with great accuracy, was as revolting in his appearance as the high cast fakeers had been pleasing. A number of natives had gathered about our camp fire and I had given them some illustrations of my own skill. They seemed puzzled, but were not specially curious. One of them stole away, and after some minutes returned with her own conjurer, the witch doctor in question.

After considerable solicitation from the natives, the intricacies of which my knowledge of the Zulu language did not enable me to penetrate, the conjuror, who at first seemed reluctant to give his consent to an exhibition of his powers before me, took a knob kerry, or club, and fastened it at the end of a thong of rawhide about two feet long. A young native, tall and athletic, whose eyes appeared to be fixed upon those of the conjurer with an apprehensive steadfastness, took his own knob kerry and fastened it at the end of a similar thong of hide. The two then stood about six feet apart in the full glare of the fire and began, all the while in silence, to whirl their knob kerrys about their heads. When the clubs passed in their swift flight in a flash struck from one to the other, and then there came an explosion which burst the young man's knob kerry in pieces, and he fell to the ground apparently lifeless.

The witch doctor turned to the high grass a few feet behind us and gathered a handful of stalks. Standing in the shadow and away from there he waved with a swift motion, exactly similar to that with the clubs, the bunch of grass around the head of the young Zulu, who lay as if dead in the fire light. In a moment the grass seemed to ignite, although the witch doctor was not standing within twenty feet of the fire, and burned slowly, crackling au libly. Approaching more closely the native in the trance the conjurer waved the flaming grass gently over his figure. To my intense amazement the recumbent body slowly rose from the ground and floated upward in the air to the height of about three feet, remaining in suspension and moving up and down, according as the passes of the burning grass were slower or faster. As the grass burned out and dropped to the ground the body returned to its position on the ground, and after a few passes from the hands of the witch doctor the young Zulu leaped to his feet apparently none the worse for his wonderful experience.

My own experience in many cases has been diametrically opposed to that of Mr. Kellar.

Mr. Kellar, however, is one of the few men whose word I would implicitly believe in a matter of this sort. I know him to be an honest man and a gentleman, and having had so much travel and experience in illusionary matters, he should be a very good judge.

The South African magicians and Obi men, while much inferior to the Indian Fakeers, still occasionally do some remarkable experiments. These, however, are different. In India, if a Yogi or Fakeer fails to present peculiar performances, he simply loses his hold on the public, but an African Obi man seems to have certain peculiar and recognized duties. For example, during times of drought he must produce rain, and should there happen to be an excessively long period when rain does not fall, the inhabitants of the country suffer much from the lack of water, and their crops and cattle go wrong. If the rain does not happen to fall within a short

period of time, the inhabitants rise en masse, and, in some districts of the country, roast the man and eat him. It becomes necessary, therefore, for the Obi men to become quite adept at finding excuses that will be accepted by their savage brethren as sufficient to account for the seeming temporary failure of their powers. In order to keep their hold upon the public, they therefore play all sorts of fantastic tricks and deceptions to convince them that they have some extraordinary and miraculous force.

While traveling once in British Bechuanaland with a hunting party, we *trekked* into *Mashonaland* to the very borders of the Matabele country, so lately the scene of the war between Lo Benguelo and the chartered company's forces. Here one evening, while encamped near a Mashona village, I made the acquaintance of one of their mystery workers.

In order to establish confidence between us and to let him see that I was one of the guild, I gave some half dozen of my illusions, and then requested that in turn he would do something for me. He hesitated for quite a time, explaining that I was a very great magician, and a devil doctor of the highest order.

Finally, he said: "Come with me; what I have to show you cannot be given before all the people (alluding to my white companions), who do not understand such things. You and I are great medicine men, but my medicine will not work with these people looking on."

I solicited permission to take the interpreter along, which was finally granted.

We walked a little distance to the bank of a stream, where the Obi man picked up a small log of wood, apparently the broken branch of a tree, which was on the bank, and tossed it into the water. There was quite a current and the branch began to float rapidly down the little river. It had gone some fifteen or twenty yards when he called aloud for it to stop. It suddenly stopped. He called for it to come up the river, when it began working its way up with a slow and rather peculiar motion, bobbing up and down occasionally in the water. He again ordered it to stop, which it did. He then ordered it to sink out of sight and the log obeyed him. Again calling it to come to the surface, it bobbed up with considerable rapidity. He requested it to come nearer to us, which it did, against a strong current, and then at his command, again stopped and seemed perfectly stationary. At his direction it would sink entirely out of sight, and once, upon coming to the surface in response to a very peremptory order, it apparently jumped some six or eight inches out of the water. Then, at his final request, came up the stream to where we were standing on the bank. The old man waded out some two or three yards, picked up the little branch and handed it to me. I examined it quite carefully, and at the time could see nothing to account for what, to me, was a most remarkable and startling performance. It was, however, just at the dusk of evening, when, although I could see quite distinctly, the light was very subdued.

We camped at this place several days, as one of our party had severely hurt himself by being thrown from his horse. I had a good deal of conversation with the old man, who flattered me highly, saying that I was a great witch doctor, and intimated to me that he would like very much to exchange secrets. That if I could initiate him into the manner of producing my mysteries, he might, perhaps, make me sufficiently powerful to produce the floating log experiment. Much of this was conveyed to me by the broken sentences of the interpreter and much by pantomimic gesticulation on the part of the Voodoo man himself.

I took him to one side and explained the secret of several startling, but simple experiments. I quite won his confidence, and after a little teaching he was enabled to do a number of small feats which would, undoubtedly, very much increase his prestige with the tribe. And in turn, although with great reluctance, he showed me the secret of the floating log.

I had been the victim of a "plant." The log lying so carelessly on the bank of the river, apparently as if it had just fallen from the tree, was really a very effective, though simple contrivance, which would deceive anybody. The little branch was some fifteen or eighteen inches long, and perhaps some three or four inches in diameter, and had been hollowed so as to be quite light and make it float with great buoyancy on the water, but without much weight. The fibres of a certain reed or grass had been twisted into a very light and thin, but extremely strong thread, just the color of the muddy water and bank of the river. By two threads only, some fifty or sixty feet long, and worked by another member of the witch-finding tribe, he was able to produce results, which, at the time, seemed to me fairly miraculous.

I don't think I ever enjoyed the acquaintance of any individual more than I did that of this unlettered, but not unlearned savage. He was as shrewd and as able a humbug in his own line as I ever met. When I had gained his confidence by showing him some of my work, and giving him a few little presents, he seemed to take it as a tacit confession that we were both engaged in making our living by delicately swindling the public, and, considering me as a brother rogue, he became quite confidential.

I could not, however, make him understand that my performances were given simply with the idea of entertaining the public. *His* deceptions were given purely with the view of making his tribal comrades have an implicit belief in his supernatural powers, and he could not comprehend how any person could produce work of that character, unless it was to make others believe that it was not mere trick, but could only be produced by individuals of the nature of a demi-god.

Since then, when in India or other places, I witnessed the performances of Yogis or Spiritual mediums, and was tempted to fancy that perhaps there might be some mysterious force at work, outside of mere chicanery, I have remembered how great was my amazement at the mystery of the floating log, and how simple was its solution.

GUARDING A MAHATMA'S CAVERN.

## CHAPTER VII.

### CEYLON RUBIES.

While I was in Colombo I spent much time with the gem merchants. Every traveler who visits Ceylon is immediately besieged by the peripatetic dealers in jewelry and gems.

A peddler will offer the traveler a beautiful ring, which he will swear by the bones of all of his ancestors, is made of eighteen karat gold, and contains only the purest jewels. If the traveler should be so foolish as to purchase the ring, the chances are that he will find it is a cheap and trumpery silver ring, highly washed with gold, and that the valuable gems are only very poor paste imitations. Even where the gems are real they are usually of a very inferior quality.

A very ragged dealer one day approached me with an air of very great mystery and said that as he knew I was a judge he wished to show me some perfect stones, which were as yet uncut, and which he himself had got from the mines some weeks before. He would not even show me these gems in the presence of other people, but made a great ado about taking me to one side for fear that some of the other dealers would find out what a marvelous bargain he was giving me and raise a riot in consequence.

Upon showing me these stones I found that they were merely bits of broken glass, which had been put into a canvas bag, close enough in the texture to hold water. Several handsful of sand were then thrown in, and the bag shaken violently ; soon the bits of green and blue broken glass became dull by the action of the sand and water, and might with an ignorant person very readily pass for uncut sapphires or emeralds. I asked the dealer what he wanted for these beautiful jewels. After a great deal of palaver he told me that as I was "in the business" and knew so much, and could not by any possibility be humbugged, he would let me have them at a very moderate price. He would sell me the entire lot for one thousand rupees. I told him that it was really too small a price for such lovely jewels, and that I could not think of robbing him, but if he would like to sell them to me simply as a curiosity, in order that I might play a practical joke on some of my friends, I would give him six pence for them. The look of pained surprise which he at first tried to assume very shortly changed to a sardonic grin, when he found that I was not in the least deceived by all his mummery. I finally gave him nine pence for the lot. As a matter of fact, they were worth about two cents, as some of the bits were pieces of really beautiful colored glass bottles, which he had evidently picked up from the refuse boxes of the town.

While in Ceylon, however, I became quite an expert in judging the genuineness and value of gems.

Among other things I found out one sure way of testing the genuineness of a diamond by quite an easy and simple method. It is as follows :

Pierce a hole in a card with a needle and then look at the hole through the stone. If false you will see two holes, but if you have a real diamond, only a single hole will appear. You may also make the test in another way. Put your finger behind the stone and look at it through the diamond as through a magnifying glass. If the stone is genuine you will be unable to distinguish the grain of the skin, but with a false stone this will be plainly visible.

# CHAPTER VIII.

## THE BASKET TRICK EXPLAINED.

THE GREAT HINDOO DECEPTION FULLY EXPOSED.    IT MAY BE TWINS, "BUT THERE
ARE OTHERS!"    A DYING BOY AND A MURDEROUS FAKEER.    ROPES AND NETS.
A SWINDLE WITH A SWORD.    HOW THE BOY GETS OUT.    HOW THE PUBLIC ARE
LET IN.

Almost every traveler in India and the East has witnessed one form or another of
the celebrated basket trick.  Very nearly every band of wandering Fakeers produce
this basket illusion. It is not always given precisely the same way.

Generally, a large oval basket, closely woven, is brought out and shown to the spectators for examination.  There seems to be very little chance for trick about it.  It
is usually some four and a half feet long and perhaps eighteen inches or two feet
high.    It is very much the shape of an egg laid on its side, slightly flattened at the
top and the bottom.  In the top an oval aperture is cut, over which a cover fits
tightly.

Then a boy (or girl), perhaps from ten to sixteen years of age, is brought forward
for inspection.  The youngster has but very little clothing upon him.  Generally
nothing but the customary cloth worn around the loins and between the legs.  Sometimes the boy has his hands tied behind his back, and a handkerchief or bandage is
placed over his eyes, so as to conceal the greatest part of his face.  Ostensibly he is
blindfolded so that he will not get frightened when he sees the sword which is
to be run through him, but the real reason will be apparent further on.

He is then placed within a large net made of a platted rope or cord about the thick-
ness of an ordinary lead pencil.    After being fastened within this net, it is also occasionally tied over and around him as well.  He then stands up within the basket.  The
spectators are requested to remain at a distance of some twelve or fifteen feet, so there
may be no chance of any outside assistance.  A large sheet or shawl is thrown over
the boy, covering him and the basket completely, as illustrated by the accompanying cut.    The boy first drops on his knees and then gets lower and lower until the
sheet which covers him is on a level with the top of the basket.  Then the cover of the
basket is placed in its proper position *over the sheet* and left there for a moment or
so, while some little mummery is engaged in by the Fakeer.  He talks loudly, thwacks
the basket four or five times with a stick that he carries, and calls loudly to the boy
inside, who in turn shouts to him, and for a moment quite a little racket is kept up.
The cover of the basket is then removed,  the sheet, however, still remaining in place.
Suddenly, the Fakeer steps upon the sheet into the basket and tramples all around
him.  The sheet, of course, prevents the spectators from seeing inside the basket,
but as the Fakeer tramps and jumps up and down in every direction, the inference
is that the boy has disappeared.  The magician again places the cover on, and draws
the sheet up in such a position that the entire basket is seen.  He then takes a
sword, or something like a long fencing rapier and passes it through the basket in
various places, and seemingly in every direction thrusting it in violently, thus proving that the basket is entirely empty.

Suddenly a little shout is heard from the outside of the crowd and the little boy. who but a moment before was inside the basket, suddenly comes up and salaam respectfully to the crowd and holds out his hands or a little tin dish for *baksheesh*. The basket is thrown over the Fakeer's shoulders, and, after collecting *baksheesh*, he too, salaams and walks away to some secluded spot for new spectators.

As the little boy has thus miraculously appeared from the outside the cro\ one ever thinks of asking the old man to entirely remove the sheet and let them ʟ the basket absolutely empty. It seems very evident that the boy must have got away in some manner, or he could not have been produced from the outside.

 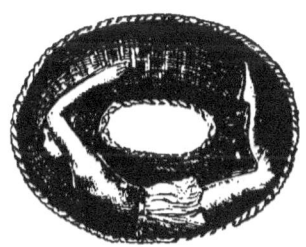

.ʼs a matter of fact, the illusion is a very simple one. When the little boy is placed in the basket his first procedure is to free himself from the rope and the sack, which, to an expert in rope tying is very simple, and offers very little difficulty.

He then coils himself around in the bulge or protruding sides of the basket, so that when the Fakeer tramples in the middle or center, he does not trample on the boy. To any one who has seen the feats of white contortionists, and how easily they can twist themselves in almost any shape, it will be evident that it is not at all difficult for a lithe and sinuous Hindoo boy to coil himself around in this space.

The sword is only put through the basket at certain prearranged places and passes between the boy's legs, between his arms and the body, between the shoulders and the body, or between the shoulders and the neck.

This I proved to my own satisfaction by borrowing the sword from the Fakeer, under the pretense that I thought it went up into the handle. I then suddenly stepped to the basket and insisted upon putting the sword through the basket, showing where I was going to put it. Had I passed the sword through the basket at that place, the boy would have been spitted like a quail ready for roasting but the Fakeer in the most peremptory manner snatched the sword from my hand and refused to allow me to use it.

But, you say, how does the boy get out of the basket, with all the crowd standing around him, and come up alive and well on the outside ?

This marvelous part of the performance you will readily understand when I ex· plain to you, *it is not the same boy at all.*

There are always a number of native spectators, household servants, passers-by, etc. While the spectators are all busily engaged in watching the performances, a confederate approaches from the outside, apparently as an innocent spectator, or seemingly one of the servants of the house. And concealed by this spectator is another boy, as nearly as possible a duplicate of the one within the basket. This second boy mingles with the crowd, and at the proper moment advances and is claimed by the Fakeer to be the boy who only a few moments before was so securely tied and ned in the basket.

I have known one or two cases where *twin* children have been used for this trick and thus produced a marvelous effect.

As the first boy, who is tied and put in the basket, usually has his features hidden with a handkerchief, it is difficult for the casual spectator to note the slight difference in the features of the two children. The basket still containing the boy that was placed in it is then thrown over the Fakeer's shoulders and he marches off to a convenient spot, placing the basket on the ground for a second or two, apparently as if to rest himself, and while he and the rest of the troupe are squatting around it, the boy escapes from his imprisonment.

Occasionally the feat is varied. After the magician has trampled within the basket and jabbed the sword through it in various places, to thus assure the spectators that it is entirely empty, he stands off some little distance and commences to blow upon a little musical instrument, something resembling a cross between a flageolette and a bagpipe. In a few seconds the basket begins to shake and vibrate, when suddenly the cover is thrown into the air and the boy steps out alive and well, entirely free from the fastenings of the rope and net, which are left within the empty basket, and are then again submitted for another examination.

This is the method in which it is generally shown to casual globe trotters, but on special occasions, where the Fakeer wishes to produce a good effect, it is given with the two boys as described.

# CHAPTER IX.

## INDIAN CONJURING.

MY SHOES PINCH AND ARE "PINCHED." MY RIGHT FOOT GETS "LEFT" AND IS
REPAIRED FOR A RUPEE. A FOOT FAKEER AND A FAKED FOOT. AN OCCULT
COLLAR AND CURIOUS CUFFS. A SOCK IN THE JEWEL BOX.

On one occasion in India, at Allahabad, an Indian Fakeer asked me to remove
one of my shoes and let him have it for an instant. I gave him the shoe from my
left foot. He took it, gave it a little throw in the air, and said, "Now, *Sahib*, put
the shoe on." I tried, and found that I could not do so without great inconvenience
and pain. He said it was because he had changed the shoe from a left to a right
one. I looked at the shoe carefully and found this to be the case; it certainly
seemed the right shoe. So I said to him, "Well, I cannot wear two shoes for the right
foot." He replied, "Nay, *Sahib*, you have got the left shoe on the right foot." At
that instant the right foot began to pain me, and upon removing the shoe from the
right foot, I found it was as he had said. I certainly had the left shoe on the right
foot, although only a few moments before, the shoes were properly placed upon my
feet. As I was about to put them on, he threw the shoes into the air and said,
"Now, put them on," and when I tried to do so I found that either the shoes had
grown immensely smaller, or my feet had grown vastly larger, because try as hard as
I could I could not force my foot into the shoe. There seemed nothing abnormal
about either the shoe or foot, but I certainly could not get them on.

I said to him, "You have ruined my shoes." He answered, "You put one rupee
in the toe of each shoe, put the shoe on, and it will fit all right." I did as
he directed. I put a rupee in the toe of each shoe and again essayed to put the
shoes on. I found they fitted me quite comfortably, and I could not feel the slightest
trace of the rupee, a large silver coin, as big as an American half dollar. I did not
wish to seem surprised, so sat there and said nothing until after the Fakeer had
taken his leave, when I slyly removed my shoes to find out what had become of the
two rupees. The shoes were all right, there were no holes or openings that I could
find, excepting at the top, but the rupees had disappeared, and I could only judge
by the sardonic grin on the face of the Fakeer, when he bid me "*salaam*," as he
walked away, that he had a very good idea where the two rupees had gone. If
he knew, he certainly kept his secret, for I never saw the rupees again.

This same Fakeer upon the following morning told my wife that "*Bellatee Mem
sahibs* dress very peculiarly." When she said "why?" he asked her if it was usual
for ladies to button their collars on with the front part behind. She said she had
never known a lady to do anything of the sort. He then held a small mirror before her face and said, "Look, *Mem sahib*," when to her great consternation her
own collar had certainly been placed on hindside before. We all laughed and
chaffed her unmercifully over it. She was about to remove her collar and tie for
the purpose of replacing them properly, when he said, "Nay, *Mem sahib*, don't
take it off." He then asked me to take my large silk handkerchief and place the

centre of it on the top of her head, and wrap the four ends loosely around her neck. He then gave a very gentle tap on the top of her head with his wand, and upon removing the silk handkerchief, her collar and tie were properly replaced.

Two years after this, on returning to India, I recognized this same Fakeer among several who appeared before me on the veranda of the Great Eastern Hotel in Calcutta. He in turn recognized me. I asked him to repeat the trick with the shoes, but he said he could not then do it, as all his powers were directed toward the performance of another trick. I said, "Very well, show me the most marvelous thing you can do." He remarked that it was not proper for the "*Bellatee Sahib*" to appear before ladies dressed as I was. I asked : "What is the matter now ?" He directed my attention to my white waistcoat, which I found was placed inside out

upon me. I was quite sure that a moment before the waistcoat had been properly upon my person, and I was about to remove my coat with a view to replacing it properly, but he requested me to take my own handkerchief, stretch it by the two corners, so as to hang like a little curtain from my chin to my waist. He then made a couple of light magical passes and said," Now, *Sahib*, everything all right." I found upon looking that my waistcoat was indeed in perfect order.

Upon my insisting that he repeat the trick with my two shoes, he said he could not, as I had no socks upon my feet. Upon glancing at my feet I found he was certainly quite correct in his statement. I am sure I was sober, for I do not use intoxicating drinks in any manner, and I am also sure that I had placed my socks upon my feet not two hours before.

I asked him if he knew where my socks were and he said yes, that I would find them in the jewel box in my room. I denied the existence of a jewel box, although at that time I had several thousand dollars' worth of valuable jewels in a small box locked in a heavy iron bound trunk in my room. When I insisted that I had no jewel box he at once began to describe the appearance of the box and told me very fully and correctly its entire contents and persisted in the statement that I would find my socks within the jewel box. I was so bewildered that for a moment or two I was fairly staggered. I took my wife and two or three other witnesses into the room and there stuffed tightly in the box were the socks which not ten minutes before I could have sworn were upon my feet.

A few mornings afterward, in exhibiting his various deceptions, he asked me to lend him a Chinese chop dollar, which he said was in my pocket. I had such a dollar, and, of course, fancied that he had seen me playing with it. As he promised to return the dollar without injury, I lent it to him. He then threw the dollar into the air and it disappeared. He then asked me to get him two of the hotel envelopes and I did so. Then he asked me to write my name in full on one of the envelopes and desired my wife to write her name upon the other one. He then said: "Now, *Sahib*, you take match and burn him." Meaning that I was to burn both of the envelopes, which I did very carefully, scattering the ashes to the winds. I was then requested to send my wife and some person with her to my room to see that no one entered. It so happened that my room was almost above the place on the veranda, where the tricks were being given. My wife went to the room, taking a lady friend with her. I then stepped in the street, where I could plainly see my wife and her lady friend at the open window. The Fakeer now said: "In what part of the room would you like the dollar to be found?" I replied that I wanted it found in my wife's trunk in her glove box. He said, "Very well, call and tell the *Mem sahib*, to open her trunk, look into the glove box, and she will find the dollar within the two envelopes which you have just burned." My wife did as directed, and upon opening her glove box found the dollar inside the two envelopes, one having her signature on it and the other having mine. I was so delighted with the performance that I gave the old man the chop dollar for his share of the entertainment.

## CHAPTER X.

### A MADRAS MIRACLE.

ICE WATER AND BOILING WATER IN ONE DISH.  A CREDULOUS WIFE.  A HUSBAND HUM-
BUGGED.  A MARVELOUS MANIFESTATION.  THE FULL SECRET EXPLAINED.

One very peculiar experiment I saw performed at Madras at the time puzzled me very much.  It was given by a very venerable Fakeer, who, whenever the members of our party laughed or indirectly ridiculed his pretentions, looked at us in an appealing sort of a way, as much as to say: "Now, do you think it possible that a respectable old man, with a long white beard like I have would swindle an innocent and guileless American?"

He had at first shown us a lot of rubbishy tricks which I had seen again and again, and which rather annoyed me, so I finally said: "Go away from here, you old rascal.  You are too lazy to show us anything really good.  Why do you show us this old stuff we have seen so many times before?"

He replied, "Nay, *Sahib*, me very good man.  *Sahib* not mean what he says; *Sahib* only mean fun.  Now me show *Sahib* something *Sahib* never seen before. *Sahib* give me one rupee I go to the bazaar; I want one brass dish.  Have not got money.  Suppose *Sahib* give me money.  Me get dish and come back."

I replied: "You must be silly.  Why, you old wretch, I never would see you or the money again."

He replied: "Suppose you like, you can keep my little boy until I come back."

I laughed and said: "I don't want your little boy.  You would not be one hundred yards down the road until the little cat would be after you."

He turned around to my wife and said: "*Mem sahib*, you tell *Sahib* me very honest man.  You tell *Sahib* give me rupee.  Me come back sure."

My wife said: "Very well, here is a rupee.  Now come back as quick as you can."

The man departed and we all laughed at her for her foolishness, and as time rolled on for two or three hours and the Fakeer did not return we chaffed her in high glee at being so silly as to be thus done out of her money.

She stuck to it, however, that it was the middle of the day and very hot and some little distance to the bazaar and that the old man would come back again in the cool of the evening.

She was quite right in her faith, for about five o'clock the old man again appeared and mildly reprimanded me for my disbelief.

So I said: "Very well, here is another rupee for being honest.  Now let us see what you are going to do, but if it is not something new and interesting I will have the servants throw you and your traps out of the yard."

He replied: "All right, *Sahib*.  This all right," and asked me to command one of the servants to bring a pitcher full of cold water.  This was done and water fresh from the drinking fountain procured.  He then poured about a quart or less of this into a large basin which he had purchased at the bazaar.  He now placed the basin on the "stoop" in front of me and said: "Will *Sahib* put his hand in the water?" I did so, and found it quite cool. He then asked me to let one of the servants put a little ice in to make it "more cold." This also was done and the water was quite icy to the touch. He also asked me to lend him my handkerchief, which I did. He laid a little stick or wand across the middle of the basin so that the handkerchief would not fall into the water, and placed my handkerchief lightly over the top. The basin was barely covered, as my handkerchief was not large, and I could distinctly see the basin through the thin silk at the top, while the sides, not being covered at all were plainly visible. He then commenced waving his hand over the basin, muttering some sort of an incantation, and said: "Pull off handkerchief and put your hand in water." This I did, and to my great surprise found the water scalding hot. Every one else was anxious to test the truth of the matter and each and every one put their hands into the basin.

I admitted my complete bewilderment and gave the old man a couple of rupees, with which he was greatly satisfied, but as he was taking the basin away a thought suddenly came to me and I offered him two more rupees for the basin if he would sell it to me.

This at first he refused to do.

The more I thought the matter over, the more I was quite sure I had discovered the secret. But I considered that the old man had fairly earned the two rupees by the clever way in which he had humbugged me and I was so delighted in discovering what I felt sure was the solution to the trick that I gave the old man another rupee, and taking him a little to one side hastily drew a small diagram on a piece of paper and said to him: "This is the way the trick is done."

He smiled rather gravely and said: "*Sahib* is a great magician. He knows everything. It is useless to try and deceive him. If you will give me five rupees you can have the basin."

This was done and to my very great gratification I found that I was quite right.

The accompanying diagram will show how the basin was made.

Of course, when placed in front of us, it seemed entirely free from deception of any sort, and as it was only some seven or eight feet from us and was handled so freely by the old man, there seemed no possible chance of illusion about it.

When the cold water was placed in it, not a drop left the basin, but when my handkerchief was thrown over the basin he dextrously removed a little plug of wax at the letter "A" in the diagram and also another little plug of wax at the letter "B." The compartment marked "C" was empty, and the cold water flowing through the little hole filled it completely in a short time. The compartment "D" had been filled with boiling hot water before we were called on the veranda to witness the Fakeer's work, and the adroit removal of a tiny plug or cork as he was adjusting the handkerchief allowed the hot water to flow in and fill the basin, after the cold water had emptied itself into the compartment "C."

It was very cleverly done, and is another instance of the cases where travelers say. "But these things are done in the open air, there is no chance for traps or tricks of any kind."

In this case the trick being produced in the open air and within a very short distance of us made it seem decidedly wonderful, but as a stage trick, if on the programme of any modern magician, it would be quite a failure.

It must be remembered that, as a rule, the performances of the Fakeers are generally only given before an audience of a dozen or so, and a trick which is very telling under those circumstances would fall quite flat if given on the stage before a large audience in a modern theatre.

Most travelers seem to think that because the Indian illusions are given in the open air, without any stage accessories, that it makes the performance more wonderful, but, as a veritable fact, the very absence of stage paraphernalia is often a benefit to the performer.

There are usually two or three of his assistants standing around and in the background who assist him, and very often a large sheet or shawl or covering of some sort is thrown over their apparatus just at the critical time, hiding it as effectively from the gaze of the spectator as an European magician's apparatus would be sheltered from the view of his audience if the curtain was lowered while he alone stood on the outside.

Prof. Max Muller, professor of ancient languages at Oxford University, and who is at present the greatest authority on earth in Oriental literature, in a conversation with an acquaintance of mine, distinctly stated that he had examined a great number of books and manuscripts, extending backward over a period of some hundreds of years, and in none of the Hindoo or Aryan writings could he find any mention of the performances of the Fakeers or the doings of the Mahatmas. The conclusion he comes to is that the work of the supposed Mahatmas is all trickery and not regarded as worthy of mention in Indian native history.

A NATIVE OF THE SOLOMAN ISLANDS.

## CHAPTER XI.

### EGYPTIAN SORCERERS.

MOSES AND PHARAOH.  ANCIENT SNAKE STORIES.  AN EGYPTIAN ELECTRO-BIOLOGIST.
NECROMANCY ON THE NILE.  SNAKE SORCERY AND CANE CONJURATION.  MY HAT
FULL OF SNAKES.

Modern travelers seldom speak of the performances of Egyptian magicians as being comparable with the work of their Indian confreres, but while in Cairo, at Shepard's Hotel, I saw many feats produced by the magicians, which were almost or quite as startling as those given by the Indian Fakeers.

Sitting one morning on the veranda, an aged magician approached and asked permission to perform some of his tricks.  As I was in a humor to be amused I told him to go ahead.  He asked me to loan him the walking stick which I carried.  He waved it over his head two or three times and exclaimed: "No good; too big; can't do," and handed the stick back to me, which, as I grasped it, changed into a loathsome, wriggling snake in my hand.  Of course, I immediately dropped it.  The magician smiled, picked up the snake by the middle, whirled it around in the air, and handed it back to me.  As I refused to take it, he said, "all right, no bite," and behold it was my stick.

On another occasion a magician borrowed my handkerchief and tied four or five knots in it, and then asked me to tie two or three knots, which I did.  Pulling a long hair from the head of a female assistant who stood near him, he tied the hair around the handkerchief to make it into a compact little ball, and asked me to throw the ball into the air.  I did so.  He caught it dextrously on the end of a little stick, gave it a slight twirl, and in front of my very eyes I could see the knots untying and the handkerchief was restored to me free from knots and showing hardly a sign of being even wrinkled.

At another time the same old man took a small metal plate, something like an American pie plate, started it whirling on the end of a stick, which he then held high in the air and asked me to throw a small silver or copper coin into the dish.  I did so.  I could hear it distinctly rattle as it fell into the dish.  Whenever he requested the coin would rattle and become visible, but instantly at his command, the coin would disappear from the whirling bowl.  As a matter of course, I never saw the coin again, but I saw the magician shortly afterward enter the bazaar and emerge with a quantity of food, so I concluded that in some manner, occult or otherwise, the old Fakeer had become possessed of my coin.

Another time, he took a round stick about four feet long, apparently a broom handle, balanced it on his finger, and raised the finger aloft over his head.  Suddenly the stick changed into a writhing, twisting snake, the viper standing on its tail with its head upright in the air and hissing furiously while balanced erect on the old man's finger.

As I stepped back in a mild fright, the old man said, "No be afraid, him only stick"; and, upon looking again, the snake had changed back into the broomstick.

Once, when I was rather ridiculing his work, he intimated to me that I had been dining too heartily, and perhaps had been indulging freely in champagne. When I asked him why he thought so, he said it was because I had snakes in my hat, and upon the hat being removed, two or three small, but extremely vicious looking, snakes dropped out of it.

## CHAPTER XII

A FAKEER'S "FAKE" FUNERAL. A BOGUS BURIAL. THE ENTRANCED CORPSE AND
A CAVERNOUS COFFIN. HOW IT IS ALL DONE.

On one of my trips in Southern India, while proceeding from Punnah to Rewah, one day our party reached the dak bungalo about 4 o'clock in the afternoon. Some seventy-five or a hundred yards away from the bungalo were a party of Fakeers, who had made a temporary stopping place near a large banyan tree. Our party was much entertained by their performances.

Finally the Fakeers suggested that one of their number be buried alive. A grave between five and six feet deep was speedily excavated in the soil. The grave was made between seven and eight feet long and about two feet six inches wide at the top, and for about four feet in depth was quite perpendicular. Then a little projection was allowed, and the balance of the grave to a distance of about two feet in depth was not quite two feet wide.

The Fakeer who proposed to be buried was apparently hypnotized, became rigid and stiff, and was then wrapped in a cloth and placed in the grave. Then across the little shelves, as it were, on each side of the grave, some thin planks were laid, so that when the grave was filled in, the earth would not come in contact with his body. The soil was then replaced to the depth of about six or seven inches when one of the Hindoos jumped into the grave, and trampled the earth down solidly and heavily, and as each five or six inches were filled in this was repeated and the soil packed as tightly as possible by the naked feet of the Fakeer's assistants, until finally the entire grave was completed, and it certainly seemed as if he was laid away for his final rest.

I asked how long the man would remain there, and was told "as long as *Sahib* pleases." I finally said we would let him remain there until the morrow morning, and it was arranged with our party that we should take such watch during the night as would prevent the grave being disturbed. In the morning, shortly after breakfast, it was decided to open the grave, which was done. It certainly bore no appearance of having been disturbed in the least; in fact, certain marks and fastenings which we had placed upon it to prevent it being tampered with were exactly as they had been left. But to our surprise, when reaching the bottom of the grave and removing the planks, the Fakeer was not there, and while I was looking at the empty grave in thorough amazement as to where the man could have disappeared, I suddenly felt a light touch on my shoulder, and, on looking around, the Fakeer stood before me in simple humility, bowing almost to the ground, with his hands clasped in front of his forehead, making the customary salutation of "salaam, *Sahib*," and petitioning for *baksheesh*.

The diagrams and engravings on next page will show exactly how the apparent miracle had been caused.

The grave was purposely made large and roomy, but apparently as if merely in the haste of digging it and without any design in the matter.

When the first soil was thrown in upon the planks covering the Fakeer, the noise made by the falling clods prevented the onlookers from hearing any movement on his part. He simply broke through the small division of earth separating him from an adjoining excavation, and which allowed him to have plenty of air. It then became apparent why the Hindoos so carefully packed the soil in with their feet every five or six inches. The noise made by their trampling feet and the crush of the spade was sufficient to cover the noise and movement of the Fakeer as he

crawled into the adjoining cavity and made his way gently into a hollow tree, whence, after everybody had retired at night, he emerged and slept the sleep of the just, surrounded by his virtuous and guileless family. The thing was very cleverly arranged, and as the route was one often frequented by travelers the dak bungalo was much occupied. Thus a very good harvest was made over the *Bellatee Sahibs* who passed that way, as the performance of the feat was always liberally rewarded.

As a matter of fact the *kansamah* in charge of the dak bungalo really "stood in" with the Fakeers, and got his share of the proceeds for exciting the curiosity of English people until they were anxious to witness the proceeding.

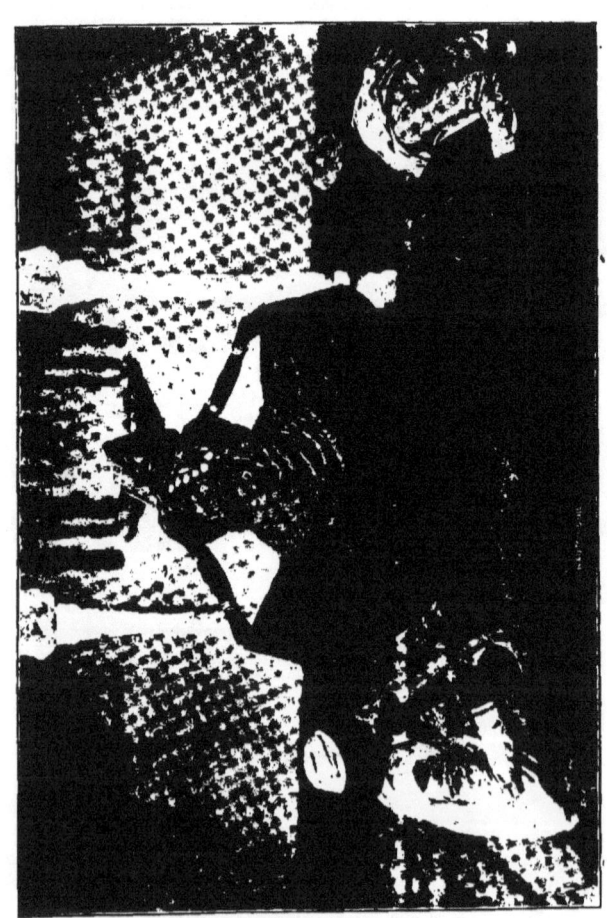

INDIAN DANCING GIRL AND MUSICIANS.

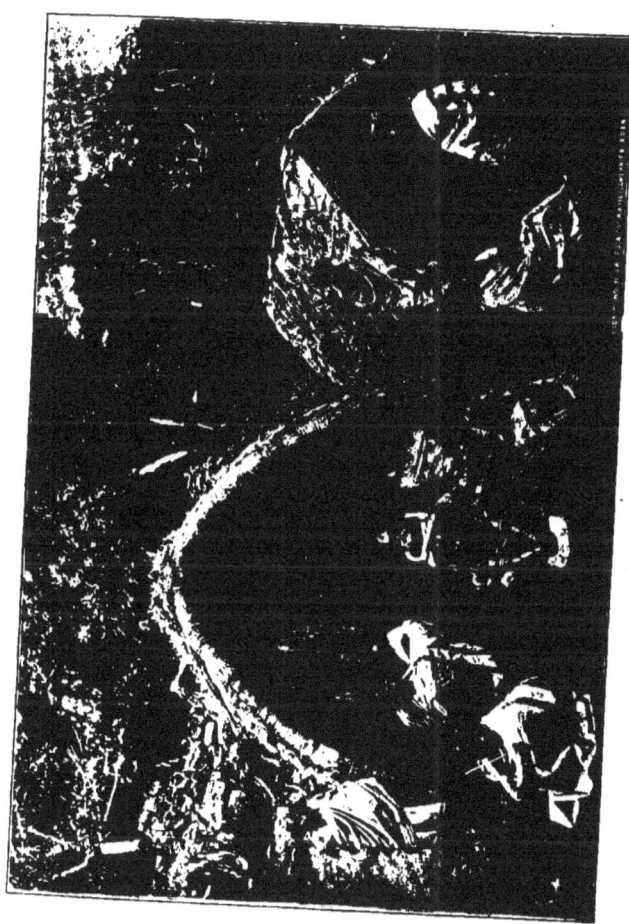

TODA MUND VILLAGE.

## CHAPTER XIII.

### THE GREAT MANGO TRICK.

One day in India I said to a Fakeer who had just performed the Mango trick before me, and who seemed extremely pleased because I gave him a couple of rupees, "Why do you always bring forth the Mango tree? Why do you not sometimes vary your performance by producing a young palm, or a tea plant, or a banyan tree? If you will grow for me a little apple or oak tree I will give you ten rupees."

His reply was, "Nay, *Sahib*, cannot do. Mango tree the only one can make."

This set me thinking. It was evidently obvious that if the Mango tree was grown by some supernatural power, the production of any other tree would be possible. And if a trick, as it assuredly was, the very fact of the Mango tree being *the only one* that could be used, must in some way furnish a clue to the solution of the deception.

I may say here, that almost all of the Indian Fakeers will, if five or ten rupees are offered them, by people whom they know are merely transient travelers (as they knew I was), explain and teach the secret of their best illusions.

Individually I rarely ever paid to have the secret of anything shown me. Most of their work, to an expert in this line like myself, is not very hard to find out, and it was rather interesting than otherwise to run across a problem somewhat difficult to solve.

I had been rather puzzled by the growth of the Mango tree, hence asked the question above quoted.

After I received the Fakeer's answer, I got a small branch from a Mango tree and examined the leaf and branch carefully.

I found that the leaf and the twigs and little branches were tough and pliable, almost like leather.

If carefully done, the leaves could be rolled or folded upon each other, so as to occupy a very small space, and when rolled out would show little or no trace of the folding.

In brief, the Mango tree is the only one of which the leaves and twigs can be folded and carried in a very small space and afterward be made to assume the proper shape.

As the trick is usually given, the Indian procures a quart or so of sand or soil and a little tin pot of water.

He proceeds to squat down at a distance of some three or four yards, and pouring a little water on the soil, compresses it and heaps it up into a little mound, practically of mud. Dry earth alone is seldom used, as the little mound would fall apart, and not lend itself so readily to the trick.

This small mound is then covered for a moment with a large cloth, some four or five feet square, which the Indian produces from the little bag he carries with him, or which is handed to him by an assistant.

He places his hands and arms underneath the cloth. It is evident to the spectator, as the man is almost nude, and as the arms are quite naked, that there can be nothing concealed, so he is allowed to work away at the mound of earth for some little time.

It must be remembered, however, that all this time his hands and arms, as far as the elbows, are entirely concealed by the cloth.

After having arranged things to his satisfaction, he stands off a little distance, makes some little palaver, muttering charm words, etc., and then pulls the cloth off.

From the center of the heap of moistened earth is seen the sprout and two little leaves of a young Mango plant.

After the auditors have sufficiently expressed their wonder this plant is again covered with the cloth, and again the man works away for a moment or so with his hands and arms hidden under the cloth. This time, when the cloth is raised, the tree has grown some five or six inches. The operations, as here described, are then repeated with more or less similarity until the plant has grown thirteen or fourteen

inches high, and sometimes to the height of two or three feet, seldom more, although on very rare occasions I have seen the plant four or five feet high.

Its secret is very simple.

The magician, like all other experts in his line, does not always use the same method. He has several ways of performing the trick. The one generally used is quite easy to understand.

The magician conceals within his hand, and while he is putting the dirt into a heap, a large mango seed. The mango seed, it must be remembered, is two inches long (sometimes more) and an inch or two broad, resembling somewhat the long razor back mussel shells found upon the sea shore.

Within this seed, carefully rolled and put together, is a young mango plant eight or nine inches long, which is generally taken from the ground with a little root and soil attached, so as to be shown to any skeptical individual who may doubt that it is a genuine growth.

When first uncovered, only an inch or so of the plant is seen, but when it is again covered the Fakeer manipulates two or three inches more from within the hollow seed.

When it is necessary to produce a larger plant, the cloth, as handed to the Fakeer by the assistant, contains the larger mango plant doubled and fastened together in a very small space, concealed within a fold of the cloth.

It is not easy to explain in a written description like this, the exact *modus operandi* of the matter, but after seeing it two or three times it is quite easy to understand the solution

To prove my theory of the matter, after I had thoroughly worked it out in my own mind, I called one of the Fakeers to my room at the hotel and told him that as I was going away that day, I would promise him not to let any one in the hotel or the residents know how the trick was produced, and I would give him five rupees to show me exactly how it was done. He explained it and carried out the various deceptions almost exactly as I have described them here.

To show also that this theory is quite correct, I here append an article from *Science Siftings* of London, which appeared in January, 1892.

It says:

"Indian jugglery was recently the subject of much interesting press discussion. One party took the view that it is only clever legerdemain, and the other that the remarkable feats are due to the occult or hypnotism. The particular trick that excited all this controversy was the celebrated mango delusion. Among others, Dr. Andrew Wilson maintained that it was unsafe to assume the inexplicable theory of matters until we had exhausted the probabilities which lie at our doors; and he said the same thing concerning a recent boom in ghosts and ghost seeing. Most things come to those who live long enough to wait, and, after the receipt of many letters regarding Indian jugglery, Dr. Wilson tells us that he has at last been favored with what he thinks is the true explanation of the mango trick. This trick consists in the juggler causing a mango plant to grow out of a pot containing earth, amid which a mango seed has been planted. As far as he can discover, there exists various modifications of the trick; for some correspondents declare that it is not a mango which grows out of the pot, but only a branch of some tree which the juggler has plucked off close by the scene of his operations. The typical trick, however, shows a mango plant growing bit by bit as the juggler performs.

"An old Anglo-Indian now writes that he does not agree with the explanation of Herr Hermann, who said the growing plant trick was performed through the performer concealing the pot, with the plant in it, under his robe. In 1865 this correspondent was on the point of leaving Calcutta, when some native jugglers came on board the steamer to give an exhibition of their powers. The surroundings were thus very unfavorable for the performance of anything but a very dextrous trick, and the mango exhibition was given on the bare deck. The performer was almost naked, so that there was no opportunity for the concealment of a flower pot under a robe. He placed before him, first of all, a small flat native wicker-work basket such as snakes are carried in. This was filled with earth. A mango seed was then produced. It was a very large one—a point, this, of importance in view of what follows—and was duly placed in the earth and covered up. The earth was watered, and the basket in its turn concealed by a small cotton cloth. Then began the usual mutterings and incantations, while the earth was again sprinkled with water and stirred with the fingers of the operator. After a few minutes, interval the juggler lifted the cloth and showed to the spectators two small mango leaves appearing above the surface of the earth.

"The basket was once more covered up, the watering of the earth and the incantations proceeded, and, in a short time, when the cloth was removed, a mango plant, seven inches or eight inches high, and bearing four or five leaves, was disclosed to view. After another interval, a seedling mango appeared, at least thirteen inches high, and bearing seven or eight leaves. Here the performance ended. Curiosity was rife, of course, regarding the juggler's *modus operandi*, and Dr. Wilson's correspondent, anxious to know how the trick was performed, offered the juggler a good round sum of money for the disclosure of his secret. After some hesitation the man consented to reveal his art, stipulating that his revelation should be conducted in a secluded spot. A cabin on a ship was offered and accepted as a suitable place, and the juggler and his questioner retired thereto. The basket was prepared as before, and the mango seed was handed round. It was, as before, a large one.

"On its being returned to the juggler, he pressed one end of the seed with his long finger-nail, when the seed opened. Two small leaves, those first seen in the deck

trick, were then withdrawn from the seed, and next in order came forth the stem with four leaves. Ultimately, the full thirteen inches of the plant were manipulated out of the seed before the eyes of the spectators. The seed was, in fact, a hollow one, and the young plant had been dextrously folded within its compass. It is the art of folding the plant inside the seed which constitutes the essence of the trick.

"A simple experiment shows how the conditions of this trick can be realized, and forever disproves any connection between it and occult science. Most leaves can be so folded that, when liberated from the pressure, they spring back to their original shape. The folding, however, must be done in a special and careful manner. The *upper* surface of the leaf must be folded on itself, and that surface, skilfully treated and watered, will scarcely show a crease on a superficial examination. The creasing which the under surface will show is, of course, concealed from the spectators' view."

One of the most peculiar tricks I saw in India, and one which at first puzzled me fully as much as anything I have ever seen, was very simple when I found out the solution.

I was at Cawnpore, the town so well known for the awful massacre which took place there during the mutiny.

One of the traveling Fakeers, after asking permission to show us what he could do, produced a little tin pail or bucket, which would hold about two quarts of water. The sort of pail which in America is called a "billy."

This pail he first allowed us to examine, then filled it with clean water and squatted himself on the ground some six or eight feet away from where we were sitting.

From the bag full of tricks which all these Fakeers carry he next produced a handful of dry sand.

Holding his hand extended before me he blew a little sharp puff, and the sand was blown hither and thither, showing it to be very dry.

He then carefully placed this handful of sand in the bottom of the pail on one side. A handful of dry pulverized brick dust was now produced and when we were convinced that it was dry as powder, this also was placed in the pail.

Looking into the pail through the clear water we could see the little heap of sand on one side and the brick dust on the other. He then wiped his hands perfectly clean and showed that the open hands contained nothing, and placing his hand within the water, he pulled out a handful of the sand and showed it to us just as dry as it was before being placed within the bucket of water.

Extending his hand he blew sharply on it and the sand flew in every direction. The same operation was repeated with the brick dust.

His little magic wand was then brought forth and the water in the bucket stirred quite sharply. The little brick dust remaining in the bottom floated to the top and lay upon the water like a curtain, concealing everything and making it impossible to see the bottom of the bucket.

His assistant next brought out a little oval piece of brick about the size and shape of a large quail's egg.

This was handed around for examination and proved to be nothing but a little piece of burnt brick, which had been cut and scraped into the required shape.

This little egg was taken in the tips of his fingers, held at arm's length from the body, and slowly deposited within the pail, where it lay at the bottom.

He now explained that he would play a tune upon a little wind instrument, which was a sort of cross between a modern flageolette and a Scotch bagpipe.

Then commenced a little incantation scene on a small scale. He would play for a few seconds upon the flute and then in the most pathetic tones adjure the little egg to come forth.

He called it Bombay Rawm Sammi, and explained to it, so that we all could hear, that if Bombay Rawm Sammi would come out and obey him and make the experiment a big success the rich *Sahib* would give at least five rupees.

He moved a little further away from the tin kettle, and after a minute or two of this conjuration there was a sudden little sharp stir in the bottom of the pail, as if some living creature were within it, and to my great surprise the small egg jumped out of the bucket into the man's extended hand.

The trick was a very good one and I gave the man a rupee which was rather more than he expected, although he talked and sang so flippantly about getting five rupees. That little song was executed with a view of touching my obdurate heart.

I admitted that it was a very good trick and told him I would give him another rupee to perform the latter part of it over again.

The secret of the sand and brick dust was already known to me, as I will explain later on, but I had not the slightest idea of how the little brick egg managed to jump out of the water.

I examined the egg, turned the pail upside down, but could see no possible solution. Finally I thought:

"Well, I have only seen the thing once, and all the conditions are new and unfavorable, and perhaps if I see it again I shall be able to understand how it is done." But upon asking the man to repeat the trick he refused and said that as I was a magician I should know that magicians never give the same thing twice.

However, after considerable solicitation and after he had given everything else in his repertoire and being paid liberally, he tried the egg experiment over again with the same effect and with the further result that I was more puzzled even than I was upon his first presentation.

It is rarely ever that I puzzle my brain over such things. If I do not see the *modus operandi* at once I generally sleep over it and find that next morning a happy inspiration often comes to put me on the right track.

It was so in this case.

The next day while sitting on the veranda lazily watching without any very great interest some other tricks which the Fakeer was performing for a few strangers, who had arrived over night, I became quite sure that I had solved the mystery of the egg

But being sure of the thing in one's mind, and being able to prove it with absolute certainty is an entirely different matter, so when the Fakeer approached me with the usual whine for *Baksheesh*, I said to him: "I am quite sure I have found out how you did that trick yesterday. There is a long invisible hair attached to the little egg. Your blowing on the flute and various mummeries and gesticulations are only intended to deceive us. When you wanted the egg to come to you, you simply pulled on the hair, and it jumped into your hand."

Now, when I made this remark to the Fakeer, I was quite certain that I was absolutely wrong; but my idea was to make the Fakeer believe that I fancied I knew the real solution, when as a matter of fact, I knew nothing of the sort. Hence, I purposely made the misstatement to see what he would do.

I saw by the sarcastic grin upon his face that he was delighted to think that I believed the trick was done by a long hair. No matter what my idea was he was quite satisfied for me to have any idea I pleased, so long as I had not struck the correct one, and believing by the way I spoke that I was entirely ignorant of its real solution, it made him more willing to do the trick over again, so after a little solicitation, he consented to repeat the performance, and placing the little bucket of water before us, he recommenced the experiment.

In order that I might get quite close to the bucket, I said to him:

"Let me sit close by it and pass my hand over the bucket occasionally to see that you have no hairs about it."

This he was quite willing to let me do, so I squatted down alongside of the bucket, somewhat after the fashion of the man himself; and still acting upon the pretense that I thought the performance was given by the means of an invisible thread or hair, I asked the Fakeer to move some two or three yards away, and he did as I requested.

Then followed the usual incantation, playing on the musical instrument, and the plaintive request that Bombay Rawm Sammi might jump out quickly and forcibly and show the *Bellatee Sahib* that he was entirely wrong.

Suddenly without the slightest warning to the magician I dashed my hand into the little pail of water and found that I had got hold of something. Just what I could not tell, for the magician himself was naturally very indignant at what was really an unfair action on my part, but my curiosity had got the better of me with the result as stated.

The magician made a spring for me and for a few seconds it looked as if we might have a life and death tussle. But my interpreter spoke to him rather sharply, and said that he was a fool; that I would undoubtedly pay him well as the result of my investigations, and he was silly to make such a fuss about what after all was a very simple matter.

Thus, with my hands still clinched upon the object, so that other onlookers could not see what I was holding, I went into my bedroom accompanied by the Fakeer himself, and I found that the solution to this marvel was, as in most cases, extraordinarily simple.

In order that my readers may understand how the thing was produced I will explain the entire experiment.

The pail used in this trick is about eight or nine inches high and some six inches across the top or perhaps slightly larger, containing about two quarts of water, the pail being of course somewhat deeper than it is wide.

In order to prepare the sand which he places dry in the water, and afterwards brought out dry as when it was put within the bucket, some fine, clean, sharp sand, gathered from the seashore, must be used. It must be washed carefully a number of times in hot water, so as to free it from any adhering clay or soil of any sort. It is then carefully dried in the sun for several days.

About two quarts of this sand is now placed within a clean frying pan, or what an American woman would call a skillet, and a lump of fresh lard the size of a walnut is put in the pan with it.

It is now thoroughly cooked over a hot fire, the sand being continually shaken until the lard is all slowly burned away, the result being that every little grain of sand is thoroughly covered with a slight coating of grease which is invisible to the sight and touch and at the same time renders the sand impervious to water.

When the little handful of sand is placed in the bottom of the bucket, to be shortly afterwards brought out, it is squeezed lightly together in a little lump, the grease making it adhere. Thus when it is brought out it is nearly or quite as dry as when placed within the pail.

The pulverized brick dust is treated in the same manner, and it certainly has a marvelous effect to see a handful of dry sand taken from a bucket of water and blown off the hand like so many feathers.

The most mysterious part, however, was the manner in which the egg jumped out of the bucket.

When the water was stirred thoroughly particles of the dry brick dust floated to the top and thus made a cover through which it was impossible to see.

At the time when the Fakeer brought out the last handful of sand or brick dust, he had dropped within the bucket a stiff and strong steel spring, made as shown in the accompanying engraving.

This spring was placed in the centre of the bucket and could not be seen by the spectators, as it was obscured by the brick dust floating on the water.

Of course the spectators were not aware of the introduction of the spring.

Then the little egg was produced and the Fakeer placed it carefully on the spring, so when the little catch was released, the egg could be thrown out of the bucket, a distance of some eight or ten feet.

In this case the long arm of the spring was held in its place by a small piece of rock salt. The action of the water slowly melted the salt, and in the course of some two or three minutes (or even longer), as soon as the salt was sufficiently melted, the powerful spring finally forced the diminished piece out of place and threw the little egg with considerable force from the bucket.

When the water was poured out the Fakeer, instead of catching the bucket by the handle, got it by the top and turned it over, the little spring thus dropping into his fingers.

It was very dextrously done, but was far too slow to have been presented before a large audience.

When I first grabbed the spring the Fakeer was very indignant at what was, to be candid, a most unfair action on my part, and I thoroughly sympathized with him, for, under the circumstances, I certainly had no right to do as I did. So to make amends I gave the man a present of twenty rupees. This to him was a very large sum. He was extremely delighted to get it and said to the interpreter to tell me how sorry he was that he had spoken harshly to me, and that he wished some other man would grab the spring and pay him the same amount of money every day.

After that he was very friendly to me and took a great deal of pains in explaining many of his little delicate tricks and illusions, and although some of them were extremely well done, yet I have never been more puzzled nor bewildered than at the jumping of the egg.

A MAORI CHIEF, NEW ZEALAND.

## CHAPTER XIV.
### MESMERISM AND HYPNOTISM.

(This chapter which fully teaches all mesmeric and hypnotic work was especially written for this work by Doctor Frank Baldwin.)

It is only a few years, not more than twenty five or thirty at the most, when almost every one sneered at mesmerism and hypnotism as being simply terms expressing a peculiar class of imposition or humbug. Now, almost every individual with education and intelligence, fully and freely admits the existence of hypnotic and mesmeric forces. It is only a few years ago when nine hundred and ninety-nine medical and scientific men out of every thousand sneered at mesmeric and hypnotic influences as being purely hypothetical and imaginary powers which some people fancied they possessed. Now, nine hundred and ninety nine out of every thousand scientifically educated individuals, freely and unreservedly admit the reality of hypnotic and mesmeric powers and conditions.

Doctor Jas. R. Cocke, in the *Arena* for August, 1894, in an article entitled "The Value of Hypnotism in Surgery,' deals with a number of actual and successful experiments (not merely with theories), and after having practiced hypnotism in all sorts of cases, distinctly affirms that hypnotism can and will ultimately supply the place now held in medicine by morphine and other opiates, in at least 75 to 80 per cent. of all the cases in which these or similar drugs are now used. There are many of the most eminent medical and scientific men of the times now as earnestly advocating hypnotic and mesmeric study and experiment as formerly denounced it.

No one but a superciliously arrogant ignoramus will pretend at this day and date to deny the reality of hypnotism.

There is still, however, much ignorance and many false conceptions on these subjects, and the object of these chapters on mesmerism and hypnotism will be to try to present, in as simple a manner as possible, such directions as will enable any reasonable, sensible and fairly educated person to be able to prove for himself the absolute actuality of hypnotic influence.

John Mar, of No. 30 Coburg street, Leith, Scotland, in writing to *Science Siftings*, and speaking of the power of suggestion, says:

A remarkable instance of the power of suggestion was exercised on a patient who was not hypnotised, but apparently in possession of all her faculties. A lady, who is a wonderfully sensitive subject to this influence, came under my professional charge for some slight derangement of her nervous system. If I told her a book was a watch, it became so, so far as she was concerned, an actual watch. If I put a piece of ice in her hand and told her it was boiling water, she shrieked with pain and declared that I scalded her. Every one of her senses could be imposed upon in like manner, and I have frequently controlled the action of her heart, making the pulsations slower or more rapid in accordance with the spoken suggestion. There is no doubt that if I had put a little flour in her mouth, at the same time telling her that it was strychnine and describing the symptoms of death by strychnine, she would have died with all the phenomena of poisoning by that powerful substance; or that, if I had pointed an unloaded pistol at her head, and had cried "Bang!" would have fallen dead to the floor.

Camille Flammarion, the illustrious French astronomer, in his remarkable novel "Uranie," tells us that fifteen years ago he communicated to several physicians the magnetic phenomena observed by himself in the course of many experiments. One and all denied most positively and absolutely the possibility of the facts related, but on meeting one of the same physicians at the Institute in Paris, recently, he called his attention to his denial of the phenomena. "Oh!" replied the physician, not without shrewdness, "then it was magnetism, now it is hypnotism, and it is we who study it; that is a very different thing." The astronomer wisely adds by way of impressing the moral: "Let us deny nothing positively; let us study: let us examine; the explanation will come later."

Professor Huxley says:—

"I am unaware of anything that has a right to the title of an 'impossibility,' except a contradiction in terms. * * * * * It is sufficiently obvious, not only that we are at the beginning of our knowledge of nature, instead of having arrived at the end of it, but that the limitations of our faculties are such that we never can be in a position to set bounds to the possibilities of nature."

### DEGREES OF MESMERIC POWER.

There are four stages or degrees of mesmeric control.

1st. The partial degree, in which the subject is partially or imperfectly under

A MATERIALIZATION SEANCE.

the mesmeric control of the operator. In this stage most of the mental faculties retain all or a great portion of their activity. Of the physical senses, the vision is usually weakened or impaired. The eye is no longer under the control of the subject. Sometimes the sense of hearing is also affected.

In the second, or sleep stage, the mesmeric control is complete, as far as the physical senses of the subject are concerned. The senses refuse to act, and the subject is utterly unconscious to pain. Surgical operations can be performed on the subject while in this state, but his mental faculties are not properly under the control of the operator.

In the third degree all the faculties become responsive to the mesmeric influence of the operator. The subject is, for the time being, almost or quite an irresponsible being. He sees, hears, feels, and thinks only as directed or permitted by the mesmeric operator.

In the last, or Somnomistic degree, all previously mentioned phenomena may be exhibited, and in addition to them, psycho-vision or clairvoyance.

## WHAT DR. COATES SAYS.

Dr. Coates, in his work, classes the mesmeric stages into six degrees. He says: "All phases may be developed in one subject; some may pass rapidly in the fifth or sixth stage without apparently having passed through the others. Some subjects seem to have a natural fitness for one class and not another. Those adapted for the higher phases of thought transference, or sympathetic thought reading, would be injured (that is, their powers obscured) were they placed on the public platform; while those most suited for public entertainments seldom or ever are fitted for the exhibition of the higher stages of the fourth degree, and certainly never for the fifth and sixth. This explains why the phenomena of the higher degrees have been so fugitive or unreliable. Mesmerists have endeavored to produce them, and in doing so, have injured their sensitives, not knowing that these phenomena depend more upon certain nervous conditions in the sensitive, than in the mesmeric powers possessed by the operator. * * They should remember that while their *influence* may predispose to the *development* of the higher phases of the phenomena in their subjects, it is only a development—*the faculties must be innate in the latter, by which the phenomena are expressed.*"

## WHAT IS NEEDED. THE MAGNETIC GAZE.

Miss Leigh Hunt Chandos has also published an excellent work on mesmerism. She, however, uses the term "Organic Magnetism," as synonymous with, or meaning the same as mesmerism. She says: "The primary qualifications of a Magnetiser (*i. e.*, a mesmerist) are, a great and good spirit, great powers of mental concentration, and a powerful Magnetic Gaze. Passes, corporeal contact, the use of discs, wands, Magnetised substances, etc., are secondary and subservient means to the three named primary qualifications. * * * * * * * *
To make your look influential as a Magnetiser, you must cultivate the Magnetic Gaze, which is of the utmost importance, for when once the Magnetic power of the eye is developed, almost every person you meet is to a certain degree brought under your control." * * * * * * * *

## HOW TO ATTAIN THE GAZE.

"To attain a powerful magnetic gaze you must devote a certain length of time daily to gazing steadfastly at one spot. This done in the early morning, when you are not sleepy, will in time cause your eyes to become so superpositive when inactive that neither hypnotism nor the eyes of others can affect you. Such regular practice in gazing will render your eyes so Magnetic and Electric when meeting the gaze of ordinary Positive eyes, they will be Negative to yours. At the beginning of your practice you will find it difficult to gaze steadfastly for a longer period than five ....... hont winking and the eyes becoming suffused with water, but this annoyance wi.. gradually lessen, till you are enabled with ease to gaze fixedly at any given spot for even an hour or more without a waver. The physiological effect of the process is to strengthen the optic nerve and is curative to the brain. Women who are hysterical can always by this means prevent an attack and eventually remove all such tendencies. A well drawn human eye or a large round black spot on a piece of blank paper, or, better still, a glass eye will do for gazing.

"Gazing fixedly at caged animals, such as lions, tigers, etc., at zoological gardens, and at domestic animals is excellent practice. After attaining this gaze you will find that it is next to impossible for the most hardened liar to deliberately tell you a falsehood when your eyes are fixed upon his, provided you take the first look, and it be not a meaningless stare, but a clear, calm, searching, piercing gaze, of such a character that he is impressed with the belief or *feeling* that you can even read his thoughts. Some naturally possess Magnetic eyes, and if they only knew the method of cultivating the Magnetic gaze, and utilizing it, they might signalize themselves by founding a new era, as all whom they could interest in their projects would become their allies and followers."

## WHAT DELUZE SAYS.

Deluze, the great French Mesmerist, says that to mesmerise your subject you must 'remove from the patient all those persons who might occasion you any restraint; do not keep with you any but the necessary witnesses (only one if possible), and require of them not to interfere by any means in the *processes* which you may employ. 　*　　*　　*　　*　　*　　*　　*　　*　　*　　*

"Manage to have neither too much heat nor cold, so that nothing may constrain the freedom of your movements, and *take every precaution not to be interrupted during the sitting*.

"Then take your patient, sit in the most convenient manner possible, and place yourself opposite him, or her, on a seat somewhat higher, so that his knees may go

68

between yours and that your feet may be between his. First, require him to resign himself, to *think of nothing*, to banish every fear, and not to be uneasy if the action of *magnetism* produce in him momentary pain. Take his thumbs between your two fingers, so that the interior of your thumb may touch the interior of his, and fix your eyes on him. Remain from two to five minutes in this position, until you feel that an *equal heat* is established between his thumbs and yours, then draw back your hands separating them to the right and left, and turning them so that the inner surface may be on the outside, and raise them a little higher than the head ; then place them on the two shoulders, leave them there for about a minute and bring them down the arms as far as the ends of the fingers, slightly touching them. Make this pass five or six times, turning away your hands and separating them a little from the body, so as to reascend. Then place your hands above the head ; keep them there for a moment and bring them down, passing in front of the face at a distance of one or two inches as far as the pit of the stomach ; there stop for about two minutes, placing your thumbs on the pit of the stomach and the other fingers below the ribs. Then descend slowly along the body as far as the knees, and, if you can without incommoding yourself, to the extremity of the feet. Repeat the same process during the greater part of the sitting. Also approach the patient sometimes, so as to place your hands behind his shoulders and let them descend slowly along the spine to the back, and from thence on to the haunches and along the thighs so far as the knees, or even to the feet. After the first pass dispense with placing the hands on the head and make the subsequent passes on the arm. If no results are produced in half an hour, the sitting terminates."

### TO WAKE THE SUBJECT.

Captain James was a most successful mesmerist, who devoted much attention to the higher phases of psychological work. His directions how to mesmerize are of the same tenor as those of Deluze, only rather more elaborate. In explaining how to awaken a patient, he says : "The next question is how to awaken the patient. With most sensitives this is a very easy process, for merely blowing or fanning over the head and face with a few transverse passes will at once dispel sleep. Should, however, the patient experience a difficulty in opening his eyes, then with the tips of his thumbs the operator should rub firmly and briskly over the eyebrows from the root of the nose outwards towards the temples, and finish by blowing or fanning, taking special care before leaving the patient that he has evidently returned to his normal state. The patient should not be left until the operator is perfectly satisfied that he is wide awake."

### DON'T GET ALARMED.

"The patient during his sleep can frequently give valuable directions to his mesmeriser, both as to the best methods of mesmerising him and the most effective means of terminating the sleep. In some rare cases the sleep is so prolonged, in spite of all the operator's efforts to dispel it, that he is alarmed, and the patient becomes affected in his fears. ABOVE ALL THINGS THE MESMERISER SHOULD PRESERVE HIS PRESENCE OF MIND, and he may be assured that the longest sleep will end spontaneously."

### HYPNOTISM.

"Hypnotism" is second cousin to mesmerism. The word was coined by the famous Dr. Braid, of Manchester, to describe mesmeric and psychical phenomena ; but mesmerism and hypnotism are not identical—they are in many respects allied and similar, but are not in all essentials the same. To hypnotise a subject Dr. Braid says : "Take any bright object between the thumb and forefinger of the left hand ; hold it eight to fifteen inches from the eyes, at such a position above the forehead as may produce the greatest possible strain upon the eyes and the eyelids, and enable the patient to maintain a steady, fixed stare at the object. The patient must be made to understand that he must keep his eyes steadily fixed on the object. The pupils will be at first contracted, they will shortly begin to dilate, and after they have done so to a considerable extent, if the fore and middle fingers of the right hand, extended and a little separated, are carried from the object towards the eyes, most likely the eyelids will close involuntarily with a vibratory motion. If this is not the case, or the patient allows *the eyeballs to move*, desire him to begin again, giving him to understand that he is to allow the eyelids to close when the fingers are again carried to the eyes, but that the eyeballs *must* be kept fixed on the same position, and the mind riveted to the *one idea* of the object held above the eyes."

## HOW MRS. BALDWIN IS MESMERIZED.

\* \* \* \* \* \* \*

In placing Mrs. Baldwin in the mesmeric condition, Professor Baldwin does not rely entirely upon any of the methods above stated, as he has found that the means used must differ with her physical condition. Sometimes he can induce the mesmeric state by a few passes, at other times it requires all of his power and the exercise of certain methods acquired by him from the Fakeers of India.

\* \* \* \* \* \* \*

In the mesmeric experiments in the family circle do not mesmerise any one without the presence of some warm friend or relative of the subject, and *never try to mesmerise any one without their full and freely given permission.*

With good subjects the methods of Deluze, as previously given, will likely be effective. One thing is sure, a subject must either be naturally sensitive to your influence or he must be brought under it and made sensitive to it.

## CLAIRVOYANT SUBJECTS.

As has been previously indicated, out of hundreds of subjects whom you may mesmerize and bring into the first stages of the mesmeric condition, you may not find one in whom the clairvoyant condition can be induced. Pray note, and always keep in your mind, that while almost everyone can be mesmerised if time and patience be taken, and repeated and continued effort made, yet clairvoyance is a peculiar innate gift only possessed by an extremely few rarely constituted individuals, and only developed or brought out by the mesmeric process. For example, a piece of steel in its ordinary or normal condition will not attract other bits of iron or steel, but let it be magnetized and it becomes a magnet, and attracts and holds all other bits of steel that may be near it. The power was there innately, but required the contact of a magnet to develop it or bring out its hidden or dormant force. Just so with clairvoyance.

## IGNORANT PEOPLE.

Thousands of people deny the existence of a clairvoyant power. This denial is usually caused by ignorance. The skeptic having never seen an exhibition of real clairvoyance, doubts its existence. Or he may have seen an imitation or counterfeit that was claimed to be real clairvoyance, and the deception may have been so palpable as to have disgusted the investigator (who, never stopped to consider that every good thing is often counterfeited by very close and realistic imitations), and he has said: "Oh, there is nothing in clairvoyance." The testimony, however, of one scientific expert, who has given much time to long, tedious and careful investigation, is worth more than the opinion of a thousand people (even though they be intelligent and educated) who have not made a specialty of clairvoyance and psychographic force.

Dr. James Coates, whose opinions I have previously quoted, and who is probably as well, or better informed on mesmerism and kindred topics as any man on earth, and who has spent long years in close and exact investigations, says: "*Clairvoyance* is a reality. Its existence in various subjects has been proven again and again, and has been testified to by many credible witnesses, past and present, at home and abroad. To put it briefly, it is either an exhibition of gross ignorance or gross impertinence and ignorance to deny the existence of the phenomenon. Sensitives have foretold illness, death, and the recovery of patients, prescribed remedies for disease, traced stolen and strayed property. *Introvision*, or *prevision*, have been, and are, phenomena common in the experience of all mesmerists of the old school."

## HOW TO FIND A CLAIRVOYANT.

In a brochure as limited as this, it is only possible to give the briefest lessons in how to mesmerise. To get exhibitions or manifestations of clairvoyance, it is, of course, first necessary to mesmerise as many subjects as you can, and this takes time and the exercise of much mental force and labor. Having picked out your best and most sensitive subjects, then carefully, and with patience, try for proofs of clairvoyant power. Perhaps you may be so fortunate as to find a clairvoyant without great trouble. On the other hand, you may search for months and years and never find one. How many hundred millions of people have voices and try to sing, yet the really great singers of any generation, such as Adelina Patti, Christine Nillson, Marie Roze or Jenny Lind, may be counted on the fingers of one hand, so it is with good clairvoyants, with only this difference, that *good clairvoyants* are more rare than good singers. Many there be who may term themselves clairvoyants, but who only, more or less, unsuccessfully imitate rare manifestations of a force they may have heard or read of, yet have never seen. *Probably not one in a thousand of the advertising so-called clairvoyants have ever seen even the least sample of real psychological work.* The majority of the clairvoyants, second sightseers, etc., are illiterate beings, who do not even know the real meaning of the terms they use, and the titles they apply to themselves.

## A GREAT DIFFICULTY.

Professor Cadwell, an eminent American mesmerist says: "There are many who believe that it is an indication of mental or physical weakness to be a good mesmeric subject. Therefore, many people will not allow any one to try them, for fear that if they should happen to be mesmerized they will be considered weak-minded.

"As soon as the man who is being mesmerized thinks that others suppose it is an indication of a weak mind, he will at once resist all he can. There are others who are afraid that if they become mesmerized they will surely die before they come out of it, and while the mind is deeply impressed with this idea it is worse than useless to try them.

"The first, and most important lesson then, is to so talk to those you are about to mesmerize, as to set them right on these important points.

"I have never known one of my many thousands of mesmerized people to be injured by being mesmerized. It is no indication of mental or physical weakness."

Professor Cadwell further says:

"It is only when the mind is at rest, or not wholly absorbed in important business or active exercise, that it is in an impressive or receptive state, and in condition to be influenced or impressed by other minds far or near.

"While a man's mind is active, he is in what we call a positive state or condition; while he is unoccupied he is in a negative state. While he is in the positive state you may not be able to make a favorable impression on his mind that would be easily made while in the negative condition. Positive and negative are only relative terms, the same as heat and cold. *A man may be positive to me to-day, and negative to me to-morrow."*

\* \* \* \* \* \* \*

Professor Cadwell's book is well worth reading, and contains much that is instructive and of great benefit to one who is really desirous of knowing the real secret, use and benefit of mesmerism. He tells very amusingly of a jeweler that he hypnotized, and says:

### HOW TO BREAK THE SPELL.

"When I became fully satisfied that he could not remove the spell, even when it was for his interest to do so, I snapped my thumb and finger, and said that he could

take them up now. I think I never saw a man more surprised. I said to him that he was a good subject for mesmerism, and that if any man ever obtained that power over him again, as some unprincipled man might do, *to simply touch the end of his tongue to the roof of his mouth, and the influence of the most powerful magnetizer would be broken in a moment. All mesmeric subjects should know this important fact.*

PRANKS OF A MODERN MAHATMA. (?)

A YOGI VISONARY.

## MESMERISM DIFFERENT FROM MAGNETISM.

"I neither mesmerized nor psychologized the man. I simply magnetized him sufficiently for that one experiment. If I had continued experimenting with him for half an hour longer I might have fully mesmerized him."

"You can remove any impression nearly every time by a slight effort, either by word or by one or two upward passes on their forehead with the ends of your fingers, or by a snap of the thumb and finger. You can throw them back into the enchanted state again in a moment generally by a word or motion. Occasionally I find those that I cannot, and I request them again to close their eyes, and possibly may have to go all over the regular process as thoroughly as though I had never seen them before.

Professor Cadwell speaks sensibly and feelingly of the taunts and insults often thrown out by illiterate boors who know nothing of mesmeric or hypnotic science. He says :

"Scores of men have come to me and demanded in the most insulting manner that I mesmerize them, then and there, or they will believe that I am a fraud. I usually treat such men with silent contempt. * * Gas is made from coal ; and the *fool* who would take a lump in his hand and go to the gas manufacturer's private office and sneeringly say, 'Change that into gas, here and now, or I shall consider you a fraud,' stands on the same level with that other fool who says, 'Mesmerize me, here and now, or I shall believe that you are a humbug.' * * *

"One very good process for new beginners is to ask all the volunteers to sit in a quiet, passive state, with their eyes closed for a few minutes, during which time you may continue to talk in a steady, earnest tone of voice ; if you do not wish to talk, low, soft music will greatly hasten the results.

"At the expiration of, say four or five minutes, ask some one of your volunteers to stand up, and it is best generally to commence at one end of the row ; take hold of the left hand of the subject with your right hand, ask him to again close his eyes, then press the end of your thumb tightly on the nerve, which is located about one inch above the knuckle of the third finger, and tell him to open his eyes if he can. Your tone of voice should indicate that you do not think he can open them. If he does, let the fingers of your other hand rest lightly on his forehead for a moment and move them downward over the eyes three or four times rather quickly, and again request him to open his eyes if possible. You may have to repeat this process three or four times. If you do not succeed within two minutes, let him resume his seat, and sit with closed eyes while you try each one of the others in the same way. Those who do not appear to be affected the first time may be quickly and fully controlled on the second attempt, provided they have remained sitting as requested, while you were trying the others.

"It is best to continue with some until you have full control both physically and mentally before you cease your efforts ; while others may be only partially controlled at first and fully after you have experimented with several others."

### SOMNOMANCY.

Somnomancy (*i.e.*, sleep reading or dream portrayals) is a word self coined by Professor Baldwin to name the peculiar and strange results given by Mrs. Kittie Baldwin in their public entertainments. Professor Baldwin is an illusionist, or, as the French say, an *Escamoteur*. In thus publicly admitting himself "a deceptionist," he avoids any possibility of argument with sceptics or persons who may differ with him in opinion as to how it is done. He virtually says "I am giving entertainments with the idea of mystifying and bewildering while pleasing and amusing the public. I am a skilled entertainer and theurgist, and will use all the means at my disposal to make my seances a mystery and puzzle to my audiences. I regard all means as fair and legitimate that will conduce to this end. Do not believe me if

A ZULU WARRIOR.

KAFFIR.

## MATABELE REINCARNATION.

The Hindoos are not the only people who believe in reincarnation and transmigration of the soul. The savage Matabeles, Zulus and Kaffirs also believe in transmigration.

Rev. Dr. Carnegie, speaking of their faith and morals, says :

According to their moral standard, which is low and selfish in the extreme, they believe in right and wrong, in a future state, and in rewards and punishments. It is often said by them that there are good and bad white men, and good and bad black men. Their language contains many words expressive of right and wrong, good and evil, approval for doing good, and punishment for wrong-doing. When a good man dies, according to their idea of goodness, all his relatives and friends come together to cry for him, that is, bewail his death. Every one, man and woman and child, come out of their huts, stamp up and down their yards, wailing and yelling at the pitch of their voice. It is a heart rending sight which once seen can never be forgotten.

### THE STATE AFTER DEATH.

After death the spirit enters an ox, a snake, a buffalo, or some other wild animal. Talking with the chief one day on this subject, he said that bad men had their abode in the spirit world right away in the forest in a lonely wilderness, far removed from all people, while those whom they thought good were called back by their wailing and singing relatives at the time of death, to live in and around their former dwelling.

If a man is kicked or horned by an ox or a wild animal it is the spirit of one of his relatives who had a grudge against him on earth, and now pays him back for some old score or other. In the royal circle a fixed number of pure black oxen are set apart as retaining the spirits of their ancestors and on this account they are never slaughtered, the number being replenished when the old ones die.

I tell you anything foolish or that seems untrue. Use your own common sense in estimating the value of anything I may say to you, and unless it is sensible, rational and in accord with the teachings of science, then don't believe me. In fact, it is well to distrust all I may say, and use only your own common sense as a guide—for I admit that I will illusionize you whenever I find that by so doing I can add in any way to the mystery, interest, or realism of the entertainment I am presenting for your approbation."

## ' PERFECTLY FAIR.

Nothing can be fairer or more open than the above candid declaration. Professor Baldwin does not claim to possess or exercise any supernatural powers. He refuses to argue or discuss the genuineness of his seances with anyone, but with all this he may, and likely does, have a perfect belief that there are natural forces or powers existing of which the ordinary individual, even though well educated, knows little or nothing. While refusing to argue the point, he possibly has a thorough faith in Mrs. Baldwin's somnomistic powers.

A DARK SEANCE.

Many highly educated and intelligent investigators all over the world are convinced beyond doubt that a few extremely rare individuals or sensitives possess certain mental attributes or psychological powers not common to people at large. Thousands of refined, educated and sensible people who have watched Mrs. Baldwin's seances night after night, thoroughly believe that she possesses a peculiar gift (which, however, cannot always be displayed), which enables her to correctly discern and picture events and happenings in past, present and future periods, and entirely beyond any deception, even if so desired, on her part.

In fact it is a peculiarity of The Baldwin Entertainments that vast numbers of people, who at first are very skeptical as to her powers, and who fancy that the remarkable results are produced by some extremely skilful illusion, often become most pronounced believers after witnessing the somnomancy some five or six times, as thousands of them do. To such people these few lines may be of great interest, and perhaps some benefit. Much of this little work will consist of quotations from well-known authors, purposely given to show that it is not the uneducated rabble who believe in somnomancy, but that its most ardent advocates are among highly educated and intelligent psychological students all over the world.

ZULU BEAUTIES.

The Zulu women are usually a dark brown in color. It is rarely ever that one is quite black  Any Zulu girl between the ages of 12 to 16 could give points to the *venus de medici* for beauty of physical form.  The girls are plump and their limbs are full and rounded, with no suspicion of scragginess.  Soon after they are twelve years old they are married, and at 30 to 40 are old women.

## THE ROSICRUCIANS.

The term "Rosicrucian" is applied to Mrs. Baldwin's somnomancy, because hile in India, as a student among the Ojba Brahmins and Thibetean Yogii, Pro- ssor Baldwin found that the mesmeric and hypnotic processes employed by the aamas and Gooroos were essentially the same as those used of old on the Nile. In idia and the far East there are still living certain adepts and ascetics who claim to be ritable descendants of the primitive Rosicrucians who lived and practised their eird arts in Egypt at a time when the foundation of the pyramids had yet to be id, and the infant Moses crowed and kicked in his cradle of bulrushes. Even in iis day of modern skepticism the remnants of these strange and almost extinct ople still claim to possess the singular attributes that made them a power in the ighty Pharaoh's reign.

### SOMNOMISTIC SUBJECTS VERY RARE.

Good somnomistic subjects are extremely rare. It is necessary to have easily introlled mesmeric sensitives.

There formerly was scepticism among many as to the existence at all of a mes- eric force. Some years ago everybody ridiculed the idea. Nowadays there is a fferent feeling. The ninth edition of the "Encyclopædia Britannica" says:— The attitude of society is not now hostile to investigation in this direction. Ex- riments carried out by well known scientific men have given a new interest to iychology, and caused most of the phenomena to be accepted as well-established ientific facts."

Somnomancy more nearly resembles what is generally known as clairvoy- ice, with only this difference ; the results are much more definite, more exact, and r more correct than the results obtained from the best-known and most reliable of -called clairvoyants. "Where there is so much smoke there must be some fire" an old adage, and ever since the world was created there have been a few persons ith a gift of clairvoyance, or "far seeing." The Bible is full of accounts of such ople. Dr. James Coates, in his excellent little work "How to Mesmerise," says : The prophets of Israel. or *seers*, were consulted in private macters as well as for cred things. In 1 Samuel (chap. ix.) you will find Saul, son of Kish, consulting muel the prophet (paying him a fee, too) in order that he (Saul) might learn from ie seer the whereabouts of his father's asses.

\*　　　\*　　　\*　　　\*　　　\*　　　\*

Trance. visions and inspiration were all accepted facts among these people. he evil and the good depended on the source.

### HYPNOTISM AS AN ANÆSTHETIC.

The *British Medical Journal* prints a long account of proceedings the other iy at the rooms of Messrs. Carter Brothers and Turner, dental surgeons, Leeds, here upwards of 60 of the leading medical men and dentists of the district wit- issed a series of surgical and dental operations performed under hypnotic influence dnced by Dr. Milne Bramwell, of Goole, Yorkshire, who is a master of the art of ypnotism as applied to medicine and surgery, and is shortly to publish a work on ie subject.

The object of the meeting was to show the power of hypnotism to produce ab- lute anæsthesia in very painful and severe operations. A woman. aged 25, was ypnotised at a word by Dr. Bramwell. She was told she was to submit to three eth being extracted, without pain, at the hands of Mr. Thomas Carter ; and irrlier, that she was to do anything that Mr. Carter asked her to do. This was per- icily successful. There was no expression of pain in the face, no cry, and when

A Somali Warrior

ZULU WITCH FINDER.

The Zulus in the South of Africa and Somalis in the north-eastern part of Africa are brave and warlike races. Both are believers in witchcraft. The Zulu witch finder's principal occupation is to bring rain and "smell out" witches. Should any one's cattle die of the murrain; or if one becomes ill and remains ill for some time, it is pretty well proof positive that it is the work of a witch. Then the "smeller out" goes through a number of ceremonies, and usually points out some old woman who is killed then and there. If, however, the reigning monarch wishes to get rid of some member of his family—or if he desires do away with some strong man who might raise a rebellion and oust him from throne—in that case the king quietly intimates to the "smeller out" that such a such an individual is a witch, and at the next pow-wow the obnoxious person probably "smelled out" and at once executed.

told to awake she. said she had not the least pain in the gums, nor had she felt the operation. Dr. Bramwell then hypnotized her and ordered her to leave the room and go upstairs to the waiting-room. This she did as a complete somnambulist.

The next case was that of a servant girl, M. A. W., aged 19, on whom, under the hypnotic influence induced by Dr. Bramwell, Dr. Hewetson had a fortnight previously opened and scraped freely, without knowledge or pain, a large lachrymal abscess, extending into the cheek. Furthermore, the dressing had been daily performed and the cavity freely syringed under hypnotic anæsthesia, "the healing suggestions" being given to the patient, to which Dr. Bramwell in a great measure attributes the very rapid healing, which took place in 10 days—a remarkably short space of time in a girl by no means in a good state of health.

Another case was that of a girl who was put to sleep by the following letter from Dr. Bramwell, addressed to Mr. Turner :

"BURLINGTON-CRESCENT, GOOLE, YORK.

DEAR MR. TURNER—I send you a patient with inclosed order. When you give it her she will fall asleep at once and obey your commands. J. MILNE BRAMWELL."

"Order—Go to sleep at once, by order of Dr. Bramwell, and obey Mr. Turner's commands. J. MILNE BRAMWELL."

This experiment answered perfectly. Sleep was induced at once by reading the note, and was so profound that, at the end of a lengthy operation in which 16 stumps were removed, she awoke smiling, and insisted that she had felt no pain, and what was remarkable, there was no pain in her mouth. She was found after some time reading the *Graphic* in the waiting-room as if nothing had happened. During the whole time she did everything which Mr. Turner suggested, but it was observed that there was a diminished flow of saliva, and that the corneal reflexes were absent, the breathing more noisy than ordinarily, and the pulse slower. Dr. Bramwell took occasion to explain that the next case, a boy aged 8, was a severe test, and would probably not succeed, partly because the patient was so young and chiefly because he had not attempted to produce hypnotic anæsthesia earlier than two days before. He also explained that patients require training in this form of anæsthesia, the time of training, or preparation, varying with each individual. However, he was so far hypnotized that he allowed Mr. Mayo Robinson to operate on the great toe, and removing the bony growth and part of the first phalanx with no more than a few cries towards the close of the operation, and with the result that, when questioned afterwards, he appeared to know very little of what had been done.

It was necessary in his case for Dr. Bramwell to repeat the hypnotic suggestions. Dr. Bramwell remarked that he wished to show a case that was less likely to be perfectly successful than the others, so as to enable those present to see the difficult as well as the apparently "easy," straightforward cases, "in fact," as he said, "to show his work in the rough."

The next case was a girl of 15, highly sensitive, requiring the removal of enlarged tonsils. At the request of Dr. Bramwell, Mr. Hewetson was enabled in the hypnotic state to extract each tonsil with ease, the girl, by suggestion of the hypnotiser, obeying every request of the operator, though in a state of perfect anæsthesia.

In the same way Mr. Hewetson removed a cyst, of the size of a horse bean, from the side of the nose of a young woman who was perfectly anæsthised and breathing deeply, and who, on coming round by order, protested "that the operation had not been commenced."

Mr. Turner then extracted two teeth from a man with equal success : after which Dr. Bramwell explained how his patient had been completely cured of drunkenness by hypnotic suggestions. To prove this to those present, and to show the interesting psychological results, the man was hypnotised, and in that state he was shown a glass of water ; he was told by Dr. Bramwell it was "bad beer." He was then told to awake, and the glass of water offered him by Dr. Bramwell ; he put it to his lips, and at once spat out the "offensive liquid." Other interesting phenomena were illustrated and explained by means of this patient, who was a hale, strong working-man.

Mr. T. S. Carter next extracted a very difficult impacted stump from a railway navvy as successfully as he had done in the previous case. Dr. Bramwell described how this man had been completely cured by hypnotism of very obstinate facial neuralgia, which had been produced by working in a wet cutting. On the third day of hypnotism the neuralgia had entirely disappeared (now some weeks ago), and had not returned. The man had obtained refreshing hypnotic sleep at nights, being put to sleep by his daughter through a note from Dr. Bramwell, or by a telegram. both methods succeeding perfectly.

At the conclusion of this most interesting and successful series of hypnotic experiments, a vote of thanks to Dr. Bramwell for his kindness in giving the demonstration was proposed by Mr. Scattergood, Dean of the Yorkshire College, and seconded by Mr. Pridgin Teale, who remarked that the experiments were deeply interesting, and had been marvelously successful, and said: "I feel sure that the time has now come when we shall have to recognize hypnotism as a necessary part of our study." The vote was carried by acclamation.

### HOW DO SLEEP WALKERS SEE.?

Professor Fischer describes a remarkable case observed by himself and others, when a boy at school. A young man, apparently of a hale constitution, and far from exhibiting any symptoms of nervous temperament, was habitually subject to somnambulism. His fits came on regularly about ten o'clock at night. The scene was a large apartment, containing sixty beds in four rows. He ran about violently romped, wrestled and boxed with his companions, who enjoyed the sport at his expense.

TUNISIAN FEMALE ILLUSIONIST.

Says the professor : "I can perfectly well remember that while running he  $\epsilon$ ways kept his hands before him with his fingers stretched out. He was remarkab agile, and would leap over the beds, and his companions could scarcely ever cat him. When he escaped through the door, he flew through a gallery to his own roo There he rested, frequently taking up a book and reading softly or with a lo voice, conducting—if my recollection serves me accurately—his outstretched finge over the lines. His eyes were alternately open and closed ; but even when op they were incapable of vision, being convulsively drawn upward, showing only t white.

"The general belief that somnambulists see by means of the points of the fingers, as well as the observation that, while running, our somnambulist alway carried his hands and outstretched fingers before him as if these were his organs sight, as also his reading (as it appeared to us) by means of the points of his finger led us to the idea of tying gloves upon his hands and stockings upon his legs. B sides, we had been informed that during his nightly wanderings he had been know to play at skittles—a game he was very fond of when awake—and that he had a ways accurately counted the number of pins knocked down by stretching out h fingers in a direction towards them, so correctly, indeed, that it was impossible deceive or impose upon him. In short, we seized the opportunity of his most pr found sleep and insensibility to tie on the gloves and stockings. At the usual tim he rose up and sprang out of bed ; but although we began to tease and provoke hin he did not move from the spot, and groped and tumbled about like a blind or drunke man.

"At length he perceived the cause of his distress, and took off his glove Scarcely were his hands uncovered when he started up in a lively manner, an threw the gloves with ironical indignation on the ground, making a ludicrous obse vation upon the means taken to bind him ; and then began to run about the room a usual."

## CLAIRVOYANCE OR SOMNOMANCY ?

The Rev. C. M. Barham, of Nottingham, England, is a well known experimente in hypnotism, clairvoyance, etc. In the *St. James Gazette* (London, Eng.) of Oct 10th, 1890, the following letter from Mr. Barham is printed :

"His Grace the Duke of Argyll's experiences of clairvoyancy have attracted much attentior The Duke's clairvoyant *séance*, as recorded, seems to the practiced hypnotist to have been a displa of the art of "thought transference," *rather than of the gift which is possessed by every one in ten thousand the hypnotist's subjects*. Yet, such as it was, it proved to be too much for the Duke.

True clairvoyance is startling, so far-reaching is it. The possessor of the wondrous gift possesse a key which will fit the wards of well-nigh every lock. To such, hidden things become plain an many secrets are open. There is no wonder that the power is often simulated. *Pretenders abound No calling affords greater facilities for trickery, in none does the practitioner need to be more guarded.* In the rar instances in which a subject may be found honest and trustworthy, a prize in the psychologica lottery has been gained. When I resided in Whitstable a maidservant of mine possessed this gift i a remarkable degree. At the first word of command she would fall into deep slumber, which wa accompanied by peculiar twitchings of the whole body. When in this state she could be sent mentally, of course—from one end of England to the other. On one occasion I requested her to g to Tenterden. To do this train was taken to Canterbury, thence to Ashford, and from thence a ca to the indicated place. It was noticeable—(1) that the subject required an appreciable time—pe haps half a minute—to proceed from one point to another ; (2) time could be antedated or postdate for her at will. Thus : Supposing she was to be at Ashford at 6 p. m. On my stating that the hou had struck it was so to her. At this time she did all that I required, even giving the name of th resident.

I presume it will be admitted that few people are able to remember all that is in a given roo at a moment's notice. Before going further. let me say that many hypnotic subjects have a singula aversion to silk. This girl. if touched by even a silken thread, would awake at once. At 9 o'cloc on a winter night I put her into the clairvoyant state. My wife took pencil and paper, and I bad the girl go into the drawing-room. where was a sofa with a silk cover. The room was dark. Sh sat still. To my question whether she were there. she replied. ' Yes.' Then she minutely began t describe everything in the room, until she came to the sofa. ' What is on the sofa ?' I inquired. ' l

EGYPTIAN MAGICIAN.

THE MAHARAJAH OF PATTIALA.

The Maharajah of Pattiala was so delighted with the entertainment given at his palace by Professor and Mrs. Baldwin that he gave Mrs. Baldwin a gold chain seven feet long and as thick as an ordinary lead pencil; also a beautiful diamond ring. He also gave Professor Baldwin a heavy seal ring, the stone being a brown ruby. The Maharajah has four or five wives and several hundred concubines.

can't see,' was the reply. 'Lift it, and examine carefully,' I remarked. Suddenly the clairvoyant face changed, her body twitched convulsively. and she awoke. Did she again—mentally, of course—come into contact with the silk?

Yet again. My son was at the City of London School. Just before the vacation I desired t know how he would stand in the class-list and promotion order. In order to do this I postdate the time. Again the railway journey, the cab ride, and the school was reached. The master, M: ——, was interviewed ; he had never, and has not, seen his interlocutor. Neither does he know < the singular occult influence which environed him. The numbers were given, and given correctly

One other extraordinary instance may be recorded. My brother-in-law was engaged to a lad in East Yorkshire. He had given her a diamond ring, which she had lost. This troubled them both I was written to. Times and places when the ring had last been seen were given me. The girl wa sent into hypnotic sleep. And the time was antedated to the day when the ring had last been seer With some trouble the sleeper was piloted through her journey to the North. Now a new difficult arose. I had never been to the town, did not know the house, and she was unable to find it. Cor juring up an imaginary resident, I instructed her to make the necessary inquiries. The house an the lady being found, my clairvoyante took hold of the lady's hand, watching the ring. Here an there the lady went, always accompanied by her invisible companion. At length the ring wa dropped in the orchard where the engaged couple had been helping to turn over the hay. Unfortu nately, the hay was being carted. In order to trace the lost ring. I commanded the girl to hold i tightly and to submit to any hardship rather than relinguish it. With a half smile she assented and commenced to describe her varying experience. She told how she was raked up. handed upor a pitchfork into a haycart, trodden on by clowns. and eventually deposited almost at the bottom o a heap of sweet-smelling hay in the corner of a disused cowhouse. Truth is stranger than fiction Acting upon the girl's story, a search was instituted, and the ring was found. This is no romance but a bald and disjointed record of sober facts. I could easily fill a volume with far more startling records of what may, I think, be described as extraordinary clairvoyance."

### DOINGS OF SOMNAMBULISTS.

*Pearson's Weekly* contains many narratives of the doings and actions of som nambulists from which I cull the following :

#### A SOMNOMISTIC AUTHOR.

A young French clergymen frequently arose in the middle of the night, while asleep, and wrote several sermons. Not only did he compose them, but he spent much time in making profuse grammatical and other corrections on his manuscript, which he would find perfectly legible the next morning.

#### A MIDNIGHT RIDE.

A nobleman who was subject to fits of somnambulism, was seen to leave his bedroom in the middle of the night fully equipped for riding. His servant, who had been instructed to watch lest any harm should befall him, followed him to the stable. The gentleman, having procured the key, unlocked the door, singled out his favorite horse, saddled and bridled him, and at length mounted him. The servant, seizing another horse, followed his master for several miles. The sleeper eventually returned home, put his horse in the stable, and went back to bed. He had no recollection of his midnight ride on waking in the morning.

#### THE MISSING SHIRTS.

Several years ago a Hampshire baronet was amazed to find that although he went to bed clothed as is customary, yet he invariably awoke naked in the morning. and could not find any trace of his missing garment. A great number of shirts disappeared in this inexplicable manner, and as every nook and corner in the room were searched without result, the baronet at last told one of his intimate friends, and requested him to sit in the room all night and watch developments. This the friend did, and after the baronet had for some time given audible evidence that he was asleep. the watcher was surprised to observe him get out of bed, open the door, and proceed with a quick pace along a corridor, descend the stairs, and emerge

JAPANESE LADIES.

into an open yard. Suddenly the baronet, divesting himself of his only garment, seized a pitchfork, and buried the linen in a dunghill. Afterwards he proceeded leisurely back to his bed. In the morning the baronet, incredulous at what his friend related, repaired to the dunghill, and after digging for a short time, found several shirts stowed away in this anything but pleasant receptacle.

### SOLVING THE PROBLEM.

An Amsterdam banker once requested a professor of mathematics to work out a very intricate and puzzling problem for him. The professor, thinking the matter good exercise for the intellectual faculties of his pupils, mentioned it to them, and requested them to work out the enigma. One of the students, who had pondered deeply over the intricate subject during the day, retired to bed. Some time afterwards he arose, dressed, and, seating himself at his desk, worked out the problem accurately, covering sheets of paper with algebraical figures and calculations. He had no recollection in the morning of having done so.

### THE SLEEPING MUSICIANS.

A remarkable case is given by Weinholt. A musical student was in the habit of rising in the middle of the night, and going to the piano would arrange his music and sit down and play correctly the piece before him. As showing the acute intelligence which existed in him during this sleeping state, some of his fellow-students one night watched him; and suddenly turned the music upside down. The sleeper however, detected it, quietly restored the sheet to its proper position, and went on playing. On another occasion one of the strings of the instrument being out of tune, the discordant note so jarred upon his sensibilities that he stopped his playing, took down the front of the piano, and tuned the offending note before continuing his practice.

### LIGHT IN DARKNESS.

Touching the sense of sight which is brought into play during such sleep efforts, a remarkable case is recorded of a young lady who would rise from her bed and write intelligently and legibly in complete darkness. The most curious feature in connection with her efforts was that if the least light was admitted into her room she was unable to continue. A ray from the moon passing in at her window was sufficient to disturb her. She could only continue so long as she was enveloped in perfect obscurity.

### FREAKS OF SLEEP WALKERS.

A writer in a recent number of the Washington *Star* says: There are four kinds of somnambulists. Those who can talk while sleeping, but do not walk or otherwise act. Those who walk or otherwise act while sleeping, but do not talk. Those who both act and talk while sleeping. Those who act and talk and have the sense of touch, sight, hearing and, it is alleged, in some instances, the senses of taste and smell.

This fourth kind is never found except when induced by mesmeric or hypnotic influences.

It is of the third kind that there are most queer developments, independent of voluntary external influences. Often the somnambulist will rise in the night and walk through various rooms of the house, go out on porticos, and, in some cases, on steep roofs, where he would not dare go when awake. Frequently he will leave the house and walk through street or field, and will return and go to bed without the knowledge of anything having transpired. The celebrated French physician, Bernheim, tells, in his work on "Suggestive Therapeutics," of a photographer of

EGYPTIAN WEDDING PROCESSION.

Professor and Mrs. Baldwin have been five times around the world. They have given entertainments in Gibraltar, Malta, Alexandria, Tangiers, Port Said, Cairo, Aden and Jerusalem, and have visited almost all the ports on the African coast, including Delagoa Bay and Madagascar.

CONGO TRADER'S FAMILY.

ut and finished the work on which he had been
d was astonished on finding it finished when he
ng. Painters have been known to do superior
been written and poems composed in the same

a incident occurring in his own family. His
o fond of fishing. For a number of nights in
down through a long meadow to a creek and
g on the bank and pull and tug with all his
he hired man to help him land a big fish. "I
ould break a sleep-walker of the habit to wake
bling about, and I determined to try its efficacy

a he left the house. As I passed by the wood
we got to the creek and he began tugging at his
him fall backward into about two feet of not
dly disorganized and somewhat frightened boy,
ing or otherwise in his sleep since his ducking."
r places where they would not dare to go when
are frequently done with safety has led many
selves. Ordinarily that may be true, but there
ath resulting in that way. The sleep-walker
om the fall.
t the same time, sad cases of sleep-walking oc-
w years ago. A young man of the name of
m childhood. His ramblings had always ended
nd for that reason his wife usually paid little
ies.
when he began to stay away longer at a time
as the washerwomen say. His wife determined
y. When he left his house he followed the road
, narrow pig trail leading up the river.
tangled hemlock and laurel and over stones and
f precipitous cliffs. His wife kept in sight by
hrough the trees. For more than a mile the
n large poplar tree, which had fallen with its
He walked the log until he came to a large limb
ot down and began crawling out on the limb.
screamed and called to him to wake up and
he cries, and, doubtless startled and confused
nd was drowned. He had been getting up in
ling out on that limb, jumping from there into
returning home unconscious of anything that

CHINESE HOME LIFE.

Professor and Mrs. Baldwin are the only European entertainers who have visited Pekin, the capital of the Chinese Empire. They spent three weeks in Hong Kong and a month in Shanghai. Also touched Amoy, Fuchow and the French settlements.

## CHAPTER XV.

### MYSTERIOUS DISAPPEARANCES.

"DOES THE DEVIL TAKE THEM?" JAMES WORSON IS SWALLOWED BY THE EARTH.
CHANGED INTO GAS. WILLIAMSONS LIVING DEATH. BREWSTERS BANISHMENT.

The general public can scarcely credit how many people disappear from their daily haunts without notice or warning of any sort, and forever thereafter are as completely lost as if an earthquake had swallowed them up.

No doubt many of these disappearances are entirely voluntary, but there are disappearances of another class, which remain so entirely unaccounted for as to cause decidedly unpleasant suspicions, and many of them are so weird and uncanny as to create a very uncomfortable feeling in the minds of any one who is not very courageous and bold in character.

For example, it is not many years ago since James Worson, a shoemaker of Leamington, started one morning from that town on a foot-race against time to Coventry and back. Some money was staked on the result, so three witnesses closely followed the pedestrian in a light cart. Two hours later these witnesses returned to Leamington in a condition of terror and bewilderment, relating a most incredible story.

They averred that Worson, having done his first few miles in very good form, was making capital time along the middle of a piece of straight, level road, when he suddenly stumbled, fell forward with a terrible cry, and—vanished. They were perfectly certain that he did not fall to the ground, but disappeared before reaching it. The terror-stricken witnesses, after waiting a short time, drove back to Leamington and informed the police. They were detained pending investigations, but had to be discharged, since there was no evidence against them, and no cross-examination could shake their story. A thorough search was instituted, but from that day to this no light has ever been thrown on this extraordinary occurrence.

Of course, the obvious suggestion is that these men had either murdered Worson or connived at his disappearance; but, apart from the fact that they were respectable men, and that not the slightest reason appeared for their doing either the one or the other of these things, they would surely have invented some more probable tale than this if they had had anything to conceal. It is quite possible that some of these witnesses may still be living.

Nor does this wonderful story stand alone. In the year 1854 there was living near the village of Selma, in the State of Alabama, U. S. A., a planter named Williamson. One morning in July of that year this man left his house after breakfast to give some directions to the overseer of a gang of slaves who were working in a great meadow which lay on the other side of the road. His wife stood at the door watching him, with her baby in her arms. As he crossed the road he exchanged cordial greetings with a neighbor and his son who were driving past. A minute later this neighbor—a Mr. Wrenn—recollected something which he wished to say to Mr. Williamson, and, turning his head, saw him walking slowly across the meadow towards his men. Turning his horse, he was about to call after him, when the boy at his side suddenly cried:

THE WITCH DISCOVERED.

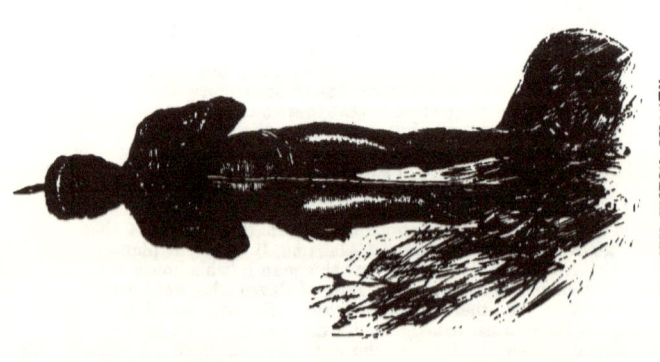

BASUTU WITCH CHASER.

"Why, father, what has become of Mr. Williamson ?"

Looking up quickly, he saw the whole wide meadow stretching before him absolutely untenanted except for the men working at the other side of it. While they were still gazing in blank astonishment—for there was no ditch, no wall, no bush even which could have concealed the missing man for a moment—Mrs. Williamson came rushing from the house with the baby still in her arms, crying wildly:

"He's gone! he's gone! what an awful thing!" and then fell to the ground unconscious. When she revived it was found that her reason was gone. This event set afloat the wildest stories among the superstitious negroes of the district, but no light was ever thrown upon the mystery. An official inquiry was held, and, after some hesitation, the Court decided that Mr. Williamson must be considered as dead, and his estate was administered accordingly.

Again, a journalist of Chicago one night came upon an old schoolfellow named Brewster, whom he had not seen for several years previously. Brewster was shabbily dressed, and bore evidences of extreme indigence ; indeed, he confessed that his despair and wretchedness had been so great as to induce him to meditate suicide. His friend, however, cheered him up, took him home with him to his rooms, gave him a first-rate supper, and put him in his own bed, promising to find some employment for him next day.

After Brewster had fallen asleep, and while the journalist was writing at a table a few feet away, a friend lodging in the same house came in for a few minutes, and seated himself at the table. The heavy breathing of Brewster at once attracted his attention, and the journalist explained his presence and what he hoped to do for him. He had hardly concluded, when suddenly the breathing ceased, and the friend, who was facing the bed, started up with a look of horror, crying:

"Good God! What has happened ?"

The bed was empty ! They rushed to it and tore off the clothes, but, though it was still warm, they found nothing between the sheets but the shirt that Brewster had worn. The missing man was never seen again, and in this case, as in the others, no explanation has ever been forthcoming. Both the witnesses of this wonderful occurrence were alive three years ago.

Another somewhat similar instance is reported from the neighborhood of Quincy, Illinois, where lived, with his wife and family, a most respectable and intelligent man named Christian Ashmore. On November 9, 1878, at about nine o'clock in the evening, his son, Charles, a boy of sixteen, took a bucket and went to fetch water from a spring a hundred yards from the house. As he did not return the family became anxious, and Mr. Ashmore, after calling several times from the door' took a lantern, and, accompanied by his eldest daughter, set out in search of his son.

A light snow had fallen, and the boy's footprints were quite distinct, but about half way to the spring the track suddenly ceased, nothing but the unbroken surface of the snow being visible in front and all around. The well was thickly coated with ice, and had certainly not been disturbed for hours.

The most careful search yielded no result, and a renewed examination of the track by the morning light only confirmed what they had already discovered—that the boy's footprints ceased suddenly and inexplicably in the midst of a perfectly open space.

Utterly incredible as they seem, these stories are all vouched for as facts. How are they to be explained ?

THE NUCKI-KA-KOOSTI AT BARODA.

The Nucki-ka-Koosti is a gladiatorial contest between trained athletes. The participants are entirely naked except a small breech clout around their loins, and often this is dispensed with. In the right hand of each fighter is held a large iron arrangement with long and sharp iron spikes, making a most awful weapon. The aim of each contestant is to cripple and wound his opponent as quickly as possible. The sharp spikes tear the flesh in ribbons and mangle the participants horribly, while the fighting ground looks like the shambles. The favorite blow which each one especially tries for is a tearing, cutting stroke in the face, which often tears away all the skin, besides breaking the nose and cutting the eyes out. These fights are seldom or ever given now-a-days, as the British Government is trying to suppress them.

## CHAPTER XVI.

## MADAME HELENA BLAVATSKY.

Almost every day of my life I am asked by some one : "What is your opinion of Madame Blavatsky?" And I would not indite the following chapter but for the reason that it is so hard in a few words to give an opinion of anyone of so peculiar a disposition and so complex a character as the late Madame Blavatsky.

I approach this subject with all the more reluctance, because Madame Blavatsky has long since passed into another stage or condition, where, if she still retains her individuality, she will have a better chance of proving the truth or falsity of her theories. Consequently, if anything I write about this lady may seem to her personal admirers to be in the least derogatory, it may be fancied that I am taking advantage of her inability to defend herself and to explain away what may seem like a traducement of her work.

I have no desire in the least to vilify Madame Blavatsky. On the contrary, she was a woman for whom, in many ways, I had the greatest admiration. Her ability and genius were so undoubted that no one who came in contact with her could help being impressed by her power, but she was from her birth an enigma to her relatives and friends.

Col. Henry S. Olcott, who for years was associated with her, once wrote : "In the whole course of my experience I have never met with so interesting and, if I may say it without offence, so eccentric a character." Another writer says : "She is one of the most remarkable psychic problems of the present time. She sets the conventionalities of society at defiance, but for brilliancy of brain power, marred by weakness and irritability of temper and indulgence in coarse language and diatribes against those who question her assertions, she stands out unique, and presents a puzzle and perplexity to those who are her firmest adherents."

It is claimed by her friends that from her childhood she was the subject of abnormal, or, spiritually speaking, mediumistic powers.

A. B. Sinnett, one of her most pronounced friends and adherents, in his work, "Incidents in the Life of Madame Blavatsky," says : "Amidst the strange double life she thus led from her earliest recollections, she would sometimes have visions of a mature protector whose imposing appearance dominated her imagination from a very early period. This protector was always the same, and his features never changed, and in after life she met him as a living man and knew him as though she had been brought up in his presence."

She was born at Ekaterinoslow, Russia, in 1831. In 1844 she journeyed with her father to London and Paris. In 1848, when she was not quite eighteen years of age, she was married to Nicephore Blavatsky, a gentleman over forty years her senior. He had been the Vice-Governor of Erivan, in Southern Russia, and was a man in good financial and social position. The difference in their ages, coupled with her eccentricity and peculiarities, made the marriage a most unhappy one, and in less

MOHAMMADAN WOMAN OF BHOPAL.

than four months she left her husband and for many years journeyed through Europe, Africa, South America, India and Central Asia, having many queer adventures and romantic incidents. She kept up but little correspondence with her friends, and but very little is known of her adventures, as she rarely ever referred to them in after life.

During this time she wrote occasionally at long intervals to her father, who was extremely fond of her, and who furnished her with sufficient money to enable her to pursue her travels and her studies. Her idea in traveling seems to have been the study of psychology and psychic phenomena generally.

She was in Europe, London and Paris in 1851. In 1852 she was in Mexico. She left there with two comrades, a Hindoo and an Englishman, for India. She visited Nepaul and attempted to visit Thibet, but for some cause or other failed.

In 1853–4 she again went to India, and this time, after much trouble and many startling incidents and escapes, visited Thibet, where, according to her own account, she met her occult guardian and shortly afterwards, by his advice, returned to Europe and joined her family, but would not live with her husband. At this period she lived mostly with a sister and an aunt.

A modern writer in speaking about her says: "While residing in Russia with her aunt her mediumistic qualities showed with great power, and the usual manifestations occurred, viz.: of raps, sounds, removal of furniture without human contact, and the reading of thoughts unexpressed by her visitors, etc., etc. In all these phenomena she remained perfectly conscious and she maintained that 'spirits' had nothing whatever to do with their production, but that they were the result of her own will and power. She was nevertheless, according to her own confession, aided by 'visible' helpers, who were never found mistaken in any single instance."

In the year 1863 she had a severe illness, which according to her own description, caused a "change of powers." She says: "Whenever I was called by name I opened my eyes upon hearing it, and was myself, my own personality in every particular. As soon as I was left alone, however, I relapsed into my usual half dreamy condition and became *somebody else*. When awake and *myself* I remembered well *who I was* in my second capacity. When *somebody else* I had no idea of who was Helena Blavatsky. I was a totally different individuality from myself, and had no connection with my actual life."

I have mentioned this much of the early history of Madame Blavatsky so that the casual reader will understand something of the incidents and surroundings through which Madame Blavatsky developed into the queer, strange, wonderful and certainly powerful woman that she was. She is generally credited with being the founder of modern theosophy, but this is not the case strictly speaking.

Dr. George Wyld, an eminent physician of Edinburgh, in his work, "Theosophy; or, Spiritual Dynamics," says: "I feel that the reading public should know that there has *always been* a Christian theosophy which must be in antagonism to that system of Hindoo cosmogony and magic vamped together by the late Madame Blavatsky. When I was president of the British branch of the Theosophical Society I at once retired from the position when Madame Blavatsky in her journal, 'The Theosophist,' used these words: 'There is no God, personal or impersonal,' for I replied, 'If there is no God there can be no Theosophy.'"

To me personally, Madame Blavatsky was a most complex character. I feel quite sure that within her own mind she deemed herself absolutely an honest woman. I am also quite sure that she thoroughly believed in the Theosophical doctrine about which she wrote so much and to which she attempted to convert the world.

I am fully convinced that she possessed abnormal clairvoyant, mesmeric and magnetic powers, and that she believed she possessed far greater powers than she really did. I am also quite sure that she had an implicit belief in the existence of the adepts and masters of whom she wrote so much. I believe that many of her clairvoyant and hypno-magnetic manifestations were genuine. But I am not at all

TAJ (OR TOMB) AT AGRA.

ALGERIAN FORTUNE TELLER.

sure that her physical manifestations, such as the precipitation of letters and the production of astral bodies, were genuine phenomena. It is only fair to say that I do believe that if Madame Blavatsky at any time was guilty of deception that it was not done from any financial standpoint, nor with a view of deliberately deceiving the public. My own idea is that Madame Blavatsky was an enthusiast and perhaps on her own particular subject almost a monomaniac. She thoroughly and implicitly believed in the tenets and doctrines which she taught, and believing so implicitly in the powers of the masters to do most anything *if they only would*, she could not understand the apathy and disbelief of others. She knew that in order to produce an interest in Theosophy and kindred subjects it was necessary to create discussion and argument. No person is so discouraging and dispiriting to the soul of an enthusiast as the one who *refuses to discuss the matter entirely*.

Madame Blavatsky felt that it was only necessary to create an interest in Theosophy to cause converts by the thousands. She was discouraged and disgusted at the absolute lack of interest that people took in her theories. The continual cry was, " Show us something material! Produce something which we can see for ourselves !" Thousands of doubting Thomases wanted not merely theories but incontrovertible proofs.

Madame Blavatsky felt that she had remarkable powers in embryo. She wanted the magnetic assistance that the companionship, sympathy and belief of others would give her. That assistance she found was difficult to get. She felt convinced in her own mind that, with time and the development to be obtained from sympathetic circles, she would ultimately be able to produce, without any chicanery whatever, the remarkable manifestations she so thoroughly believed in. She believed she was fully justified in creating an interest and a desire to discuss and talk theosophy by any means whatever at her command.

I am quite sure that her remarkable physical manifestations were produced entirely by deception. But I also firmly believe that in using such deception she was actuated solely and wholly by the desire to create an interest in Theosophy, and had no desire to deceive the public and her friends for the sake of the deception. I believe that she regretted the deception. But deemed it fully justifiable, as one of the means used to produce a certain end. She thought that if enough interest were created, that sooner or later the masters themselves would give her the power she so much desired and so fully believed in, and I am not at all sure but that as the insane person fully imagines herself Queen of the earth, or some other impossible character, that Madame Blavatsky's desire was intensified, until it became a semi-mania, in which she herself believed in the genuineness of the absolute deception she was then practising.

In 1871 Madame Blavatsky was in Alexandria, Egypt, and there met a certain Madame Coulomb. This acquaintance was a most unfortunate one for Madame Blavatsky.

In 1872 she left Egypt and went to Russia, and lived for a while at Odessa, and finally in 1873 went to Paris, and, according to her biographer, at that time "the psychic relationship between herself and her occult teachers in the East was already established on that intimate footing which has rendered her whole subsequent life subject to its practical direction."

Now, as proving the correctness of my belief that she was even then on the verge of monomania, the same writer says that she would "lose temper and time with assailants, and spend her psychic energy at the wrong places with wrong people and at the wrong moments."

In 1873 she visited New York city, and lived in America until 1879, and became a naturalized American.

In November, 1875, the Theosophical Society was formed. In America she wrote her great work, "Isis Unveiled."

BOMBAY MAIDENS.                    NAUTCH GIRL OF ULWAR.

The Orient is full of contradictions to our way of looking at things. If during a conversation the head is nodded backward and forward, in this country it signifies "yes." In the Orient it means "no," and the motion of the head which to us means "no," in that country means "yes." If you wish your horse to go faster, you chirrup to him. That same sound is made by Oriental drivers, but there it makes the horse stop instead of accelerating his gait. The dancing girls don't dance, but wriggle and shuffle lasciviously, and often disgustingly.

In 1878 she again went to India, and in 1879 organized the Theosophical Society in Bombay. Late in 1879 she became acquainted with Mr. A. P. Sinnett, who was connected with the editorial department of the Pioneer at Allahabad. Sinnett became a great admirer of Madame Blavatsky and a strong supporter of her claims. Mr. Sinnett's impressions of Madame Blavatsky at that time are as follows : " Some recall her flushed and voluble, too loudly declaiming against some person or other who had misjudged her or her society ; some show her quiet and companionable, pouring out a flood of interesting talk about Mexican antiquities, or Egypt or Peru, showing a knowledge of the most varied and far-reaching kind, and a memory for the names and places and archæological theories she would be dealing with, that was fairly fascinating to her hearers."

While in India about this time, she became acquainted with Mr. A. O. Hume. This gentleman, who held an important government position, became much interested in Madame Blavatsky, and, in company with Mr. Sinnett, organized a branch society, which was intended to secure the interest and co-operation of Anglo-Indian people. As a proof of this favorable opinion of Madame Blavatsky and Theosophy, he published a small work entitled " Hints on Esoteric Theosophy," but later on his belief in the reality of much of the phenomena was shaken by some discoveries which he made, and he withdrew entirely from the society. In a letter of his, published at the time, he said : "Despite all of the frauds perpetrated there have been genuine phenomena, and that though of a low order, Madame really had occult force of considerable though limited power behind her, that _Koot Hoomi_ is a reality, but by no means the powerful God-like being he has been painted, but he has had some share, directly or indirectly, in the production of the Koot Hoomi letters."

Even Sinnett himself admits later on that "her occult powers have become uncertain and capricious."

In 1882 she removed to a suburb of Madras called Adyar, where, in the fall of that year, she was very seriously ill, but finally became better.

In 1884 she became so ill that a voyage was taken to Europe with a hope that the sea air and the change would restore her exhausted vitality.

While in India Madame Coulomb, whom she had known in Alexandria, was engaged as housekeeper at the headquarters of the Theosophical Society. She was a married woman, and her husband seems to have been engaged with her as a general factotum, and to do work of all sorts.

Madame Coulomb was in charge of the Madras quarters while Madame Blavatsky was absent in Europe, and, for some reason or other, seemed to have made things decidedly disagreeable for the officers of the society who remained in India in charge of affairs pro tem during Madame Blavatsky's absence, and finally Coulomb and her husband were both discharged, not only from the premises of which they had charge, but were also expelled from the Theosophical Society, and, in order to get square with their assailants, they gave to the proprietors of the _Christian College Magazine_ at Madras a number of letters which had from time to time been sent to Madame Coulomb by Madame Blavatsky. These letters were mainly in reference to the production of certain occult phenomena by Madame Blavatsky, in which both Coulomb and her husband took part. Madame Coulomb also published a small pamphlet called "Some Account of my Intercourse with Madame Blavatsky, from 1872 to 1884."

It is only fair to Madame Blavatsky to say that she claimed that the letters published by Coulomb in the _Christian College Magazine_ were forgeries, but in the preface of her pamphlet Coulomb says : "I have not forged her name. I hope Madame Blavatsky will prosecute me (I shall not run away), but I do not think she will, for she knows how much would then be revealed, and how trumpery her profession would then turn out to be."

When Madame Blavatsky became fully aware of the charges and allegations made against her by the Coulombs, she declared that she would go back to India and prosecute her slanderers. She certainly did go back to India, but she certainly did *not* bring the matter into court at all or make any attempt to do so. The letters which were published, if genuine, certainly proved beyond doubt that Madame Blavatsky was guilty of an absolute and positive deception. Madame Blavatsky admitted the genuineness of a portion of the letters, but claimed that the parts which incriminated her were forgeries. It would seem, however, to the ordinary observer that if Madame Blavatsky felt quite sure that the letters were fraudulent she certainly would have instituted a criminal prosecution against the Coulombs for forgery and malicious libel as well.

Several letters, presumed to be from the Mahatmas, were sent to Mr. Sinnett and also to Mr. Hume. These letters were supposed to be from *Koot Hoomi*, and in one of them Mr. Hume's attention is directed to a certain young man. The letter states: "*A soul* is being breathed into him and new spirit let in, and every day he is advancing to a state of higher development. One fine morning the soul will find him. Unlike your English mystics, it will be in the guidance of true living adepts."

Now, Mr. Hume himself distinctly states that, "at the time the above passage was written the young man in question was systematically cheating and swindling me on false contracts, besides embezzling my money."

Toward the latter part of 1884, Madame Blavatsky returned to India, but did not institute legal proceedings of any sort against her persecutors, but so much excitement and discussion had been caused by this exposure (or, if you prefer it, "so-called" exposure), that "The Society for Psychical Research," of London, took the matter up. This society was organized for the purpose of scientifically, or by any other means, testing the genuineness of any abnormal phenomena. That is, such phenomena as might come within their reach. This society commenced a series of inquiries, and their first report (which was printed in December, 1884), speaking of Madame Blavatsky, states that, "it seems undeniable that there is a *prima facie* case for some part at least of the claims made which cannot be ignored."

A resolution was passed that in order to complete a more definite and reliable judgment it was only fair to send some "trusted observer" to India, and there to examine witnesses of all sorts, Europeans and natives, and get such reliable information as could not be obtained at long range. Mr. R. Hodgson, a well-known member of the society, went out to India in the latter part of 1884. He investigated the matter for several months and finally returned to England in April, 1885, and published the result of his investigations in December of that year.

The final report of the society, in brief, is this: "For our own part we regard her neither as a mouthpiece of hidden seers nor as a mere vulgar adventuress; we think that she has achieved a title to permanent remembrance as one of the most accomplished, ingenious and interesting impostors in history."

Among other fraudulent phenomena was the following manifestation: In 1883, on the 26th of May, Col. Olcott wrote: "Fine phenomena. Got pair of tortoise shell vases in cabinet, a moment before empty."

Madame Coulomb claimed that the vases and flowers were placed in the cabinet by herself and husband. As proving the truth of this, Mr. Hodgson called at the general store where Madame Coulomb said she had bought the vases. He was there shown the books of the firm and the entry, proving undoubtedly that the vases had been purchased by Madame Coulomb on the 25th of May, and that Col. Olcott received them by his miraculous agency on the 26th of May.

Mr. Hodgson distinctly shows that the cabinet or "shrine," as it was called, was so constructed that not only could vases and other material objects be placed within it and removed by trickery, but that a fraudulent materialization also took place by the same means.

Another undoubtedly fraudulent manifestation was one in which Mr. Sinnett claims he received a letter and documents, which he distinctly states were sent to him through occult agencies from the Great Master.

In *The Occult World*, on page 149, is printed a large portion of this letter whic': is claimed to be from the Mahatmas. As a matter of fact the greater portion of this letter is *an exact copy of a lecture which had been delivered two months before by Prof. Kiddell of New York*. This lecture was reported fully in an American newspaper and the Mahatmas who sent it to Mr. Sinnett had ample time to get a copy of the American paper and thus save themselves the trouble of composing the same.

It seems almost impossible to doubt that Madame Blavatsky thought the lecture was a good thing and took occasion to have it precipitated in the form of a letter in a place "where it would do the most good."

Another case in which Madame Blavatsky deceived her believers is as follows:

In the January number of *The Theosophist* for 1893 a most startling article was published by Madame Blavatsky under the title, "Can the 'Double' Murder?" According to Madame Blavatsky it was designed to show "the enormous potentiality of the human will upon the mesmeric subjects, so that the *double, or mayu-rupa,* when projected transcorporally will carry out the mesmeriser's mandate with helpless subserviency." She says: "It is reprinted because the evidence actually occurred and they possess a very deep interest for the student of psychological science."

In the March number was a letter from a correspondent. Madame Blavatsky in an editorial footnote says:

"We assure our learned correspondent that every word of our narrative was true."

An English author, by name William Oxley, had such thorough faith in Madame Blavatsky that he inserted the article in a book which he had published on Egypt. This insertion was made to show that psychological and mesmeric powers were used in modern as well as ancient times. The author must have got into some little difficulty over the matter, because later on in another publication he says:

"My attention was called to the statements made in my book and an explanation requested. I consulted the 'Annual Register' for that year, as well as some newspaper files, and to my astonishment found that the historical facts as given by Madame Blavatsky and the other documents referred to were at direct variance. In short, beyond the mere fact that the murders were committed, the rest of her 'actual facts' are pure fictions.

"It now appears that it was a newspaper story written for the New York *Sun* and formed one of a mystical series. And thus it comes to pass that students of psychology are presented with convictions which in their simplicity they suppose are given them to study and work out as psychological problems, and at the same time are assured that every word of the narrative is true.".

A MAHARAJAH'S PALACE.

Indian cities are crowded with beautiful palaces, temples, tombs and pagodas. The wealthy Rajahs and Maharajahs spend enormous sums in erecting lovely buildings and fitting them in the most sumptuous manner.

GOVERNMENT BUILDING AT CALCUTTA.

## CHAPTER XVII.

### A FEW WORDS ABOUT CLAIRVOYANCY.

PSYCHIC FORCES NOT SUPERNATURAL.    LIMITS TO THE POWER OF A CLAIRVOYANT.
SOMNOMANCY AND SOMNAMBULISM.    INTUITIVE PERCEPTIONS.

I am not in any sense a believer in the supernatural, but I do believe there are certain forces in nature, psychic forces I shall call them for lack of a better name, which are as yet hardly comprehended or understood by the majority, even of scientific students.

Mr. Stinson Jarvis, in a recent number of the *Arena*, says :

There is one word which may soon be erased from our mental dictionaries—the word "supernatural." We have so little further use for it. When we prove to ourselves, by scientific methods the existence of spirit and some of its powers in human beings—when we utilize it by artificial means and find that mesmerized patients can acquire knowledge through it as freely as water from a public tap—then we appreciate that spirit is as much a part of our makeup as our limbs are,—in fact, a more essential portion, for the limbs can be parted with, but that which is the life in us is the power of resisting death.

Personally, I am quite sure there are a few gifted beings who have, by nature, or perhaps have attained by mental development, some peculiar power, such as is generally called " clairvoyance."

I do not think that the possession of this power argues that the individual has anything at all that may in any way be deemed superhuman or unnatural.

People often say to me : " If there is such a thing as clairvoyance or somnomancy, what is it like ?  When your wife says, ' I see a man falling over a cliff,' or ' I see a burning house,' does she literally and actually have the vision before her, or is it merely a mental impression ?  If she is really insensible, if her eyes are really closed, how then can she see ? "

Speaking of this very thing, Mr. Jarvis in his *Arena* article says :

An advertisement appeared for a long time on the back of the London *Graphic*. In a red disc, the letters of the name " Pears " appeared in white. You looked at it for some time, the closed your eyes tightly, and afterwards the letters vividly appeared to your mind's sight in other colors. Somebody explained about the red color exciting the optic nerves, and the letters reproducing themselves through reflex action in supplemental colors. The explanation, whatever it was, sounded more learned than satisfactory. For what is "sight"?  Are there two kinds of sight, or only one ? My mesmerized patients, while asleep and with eyes closed, saw everything I saw or told them to see. Then, also, there is the sight of the eyes. But are there two kinds of sight ?  I think not. The system of nerves and lenses called the eyes seems like some delicate photographic apparatus to convey sensation or suggestion to the interior faculty, which, in both above cases, does the seeing.

The experiment as above quoted has been tried by almost every person, and nine people out of ten have the capacity to reproduce this experiment and test it for themselves, but occasionally there are a few color blind people who cannot get the results. Here then is a sight which is not a sight, a vision which is not actually beheld with the normal organs.

It is certain that when the eyes are absolutely closed that physical sight or vision cannot take place, and yet when the eyes are tightly and firmly closed, the picture of the red spot is plainly and distinctly visible, by those who possess the natural physical and mental qualifications necessary to test the reality of the experiment.

People who have lost their eyesight and become so blind as to be totally unable to distinguish day from night, often say they can quite distinctly see some particular thing they were accustomed to gaze upon while in possession of the organs of vision.

If this be so, that they see the sights claimed, it certainly must be purely a mental vision, for the physical organs are entirely destroyed.

Thus it is that the clairvoyant may see mentally, while seemingly insensible and unable to use the normal organization.

People on their deathbeds often speak of seeing green fields and beautiful sights, but it evidently is not a physical vision.

But there are a few people who, try as they may, never see the red spot excepting with their eyes wide open.

I believe that clairvoyance or somnomancy is but a further development of the ideality, which enables people to see the red spot with their closed eyes. As some people see this red spot clearly and brightly and distinctly, and as other people see it very vaguely or do not see it at all, so there are grades and conditions of clairvoyance. Some clairvoyants see a great deal. Their visions are clear and distinct. These are but few. Others see but partial sights. Their visions are vague, jumbled up, cloudy and uncertain, and there are thousands who claim to see visions (and perhaps who may delude themselves) who in reality never see anything with mental or soul eyes.

Mrs. Baldwin, when placed in the true somnomistic condition, has dreams or visions which appear before her with more or less distinctness.

It must be here understood that I do not claim in my public entertainments that my experiments are always and *absolutely genuine.*

I am an entertainer, and people come to be amused ; and, where I cannot get absolutely unimpeachable results, I must of necessity give the next best thing, and I admit that I would use illusion, simulation and deception sooner than allow my entertainment to become a failure.

This is one reason why people sometimes say to me, "I enjoyed your performance so much last night, the experiments were so startling. It seemed utterly impossible that there should be the slightest doubt about their genuineness, but to-night her replies seemed uncertain, as if they were not quite reliable."

The power of a clairvoyant is often limited.

Just as the real or normal vision may be limited by fogs, cloudy weather, dust or other things, so the spiritual or soul vision may be impaired by causes we do not understand. Atmospheric conditions, which affect the ordinary run of people so much, affect the delicate and nervous organizations of clairvoyants far more.

It is quite a common thing to hear a man say : "I have been so worried and troubled over the death of my child that I have neglected my business and forgotten many things which I should have attended to."

With clairvoyants any physical ache or pain, illness or disturbance, any mental shock, grief or worry, makes very much difference in the accuracy and reliability of their various visions.

A person with normal sight can see farther than a person who is short-sighted, yet within his range the short-sighted man's vision is just as clear and distinct as that of the man with the normal sight.

Then there are those who are termed long-sighted, and these individuals can see farther than the ordinary person. A man with a small telescope can see, perhaps, farther than any man can with ordinary sight, and the man with a large and powerful telescope can see still farther, yet with all of these individuals, from the short-sighted man to the man with the Lick telescope at his command, their vision is limited.

Just so a clairvoyant's powers are limited, and as a telescope out of order would not give good results, so a thousand and one things may happen to cause a person who is a good clairvoyant to-day to be utterly unreliable on the morrow.

My wife's visions, as near as she can remember, come to her something after the manner that dreams come to an ordinary individual.

In her "intuitive perceptions" there is not the least doubt but that she often sees a mental picture before her, but the answers as given may not only comprise this mental depictment but may include her intuitive summing up of the case and its surroundings.

There are occasions when, I must confess, her clairvoyant answers seem entirely at fault and are absolutely unreliable, and there are quite often occasions when she seems to lose her power entirely.

Like normal sleep, her power is not always at her own disposal. How many times people desire sleep and yet it will not come to ease the aching head. Often when sleep is most needed it is most conspicuous by its absence. And oftentimes when I would especially desire her results to be clear and convincing they are semi or total failures.

If genuine mental results cannot be given, then I must of necessity give the next best imitation that I can.

The necessity for deception, I am glad to say, does not arise every day, but I am always careful to candidly inform my audiences that I should be looked upon only as an entertainer of an illusionary nature who is liable at any time to cozen them.

If I can get genuine mental results, so much the better, but if I cannot get them, I am happy to say that whenever it is necessary to present a piece of escamoteric, it is always so nearly like the genuine that none but the greatest experts can tell the difference.

A true scientist will take cognizance of the smallest fact, and though the light that floats before may appear a mere will-o'-the-wisp, he will follow it until he demonstrates by careful, impartial and exhaustive investigation whether it rest on the bed-rock of truth or not, remembering that the prejudices of hoary thought and early training may blind him to sensible appreciation of the true significance of the problem that confronts him. It is not more than five years since a paper read on "Hypnotism" in the medical society of a leading city was excluded from the report of the society's meeting, on the ground that the subject was unscientific and absurd.

From present indications we are entering a new field of scientific discovery, or to be more explicit, the great body of scientific thinkers are expressing a willingness to recognize phenomena other than material, and to treat with a measure of respect the views and discoveries made by the patient heralds of psychic truths which have long been tabooed as little worthy the attention of scientific investigators, whose eyes have been accustomed to rest on the earth, its rocks, plants and animals, as the myths of bygone days. The age of electrical invention has been so marvelous that men have ceased to wonder at the inventive ingenuity of man. The age of psychological discovery upon which we are now entering, if it be unrestricted and receive the careful and unbiased attention of our best brains, will, we believe, unfold a world of truth, eclipsing in its startling character as well as in its great utility the greatest discoveries.

The committee on hypnotism of the British Medical Association reported recently affirming the genuineness of the agency and prescribing restrictions. Its use should be forbidden to all but physicians, and these should not exercise it upon patients except in the presence of relatives. It is further declared useful in relieving pain and procuring sleep, but it is not certain whether it can be made a cure for drunkenness.

## CHAPTER XVIII.
### THE KENNIAHS OF BORNEO.

The beautiful island of Borneo is inhabited by a number of savage races, the Kenniahs, Kayans, etc.

These people are unfortunately addicted to the unpleasant custom of taking off each other's head on the very slightest provocation. Often no provocation at all is necessary. The mere sight of an enemy may cause a rabid desire to become possessed of his head.

Should the head be obtained, it is always carried to the village inhabited by a savage captain, and there placed upon a high post, which serves as an adornment to the residence of the gentleman with homicidal tendencies.

In Sarawak territory, which is governed by the Rajah Brooke, the custom has nearly died out, but on rare occasions border tribes make incursions and attack the inhabitants.

In 1890 there was a raid by the Leppy Teppo Kenniahs, who live in the Balungan River district in Dutch Borneo. They attacked the Kayans of the Buram River territory, within the Rajah Brooke's domains.

The Kenniah's are an inordinately superstitious race.

An English writer in describing this raid, says :

"In accordance with their custom, some of their braves have previously spent days in the jungle away from the vast communal 'house,' while they listened for the omens—the cries of certain birds and animals—which auger success or otherwise for the expedition. No one on the march will mention the name of the people who are to be attacked, lest the 'omen birds' of the enemy might overhear and give timely warning. No warrior on whose body or limbs a fire-fly has momentarily rested, prior to the real start being made, will proceed further, for is not this an indication from the unseen powers that in that spot he will be wounded—perhaps unto death. Furthermore, after the first day's journey, the chief has caused a tree to be felled, and all those who intend seeing the matter through file past it, and give one hack at the post with their swords, while others, who up to this moment have comported themselves with the most swaggering bravado, here exhibit unmistakable signs of fear, draw back and return home, much derided by the women."

## CHAPTER XIX.

### BREAKING STONES UPON A MAN'S BODY.

A short time ago I witnessed an entertainment given in a side show on one of the English race courses. Gymnastic and acrobatic feats were given, but the principal drawing card was a feat which, to those who do not understand the secret of it, seemed absolutely miraculous.

One of the acrobats supported his feet upon two little four-legged stools and his hands upon two others, bracing his body into a stiff bridge, as in the accompanying cut. A heavy anvil was placed upon his abdomen, and another

one of the acrobats took a large sledge hammer and beat a piece of red hot iron into the shape of a horseshoe. The anvil was then removed and two very large blocks of granite were placed upon the man, and on these blocks of granite large paving stones were broken, requiring much force and heavy blows to break them.

The secret is very simple. It is really an experiment in inertia. The blows are hardly felt by the man below, the effect of them being almost absorbed by the large mass of iron and the inertia of the anvil. This is also the case where the two heavy blocks of granite are used. As a matter of fact, the larger the anvil and the more massive the blocks, the less are the blows felt by the man beneath.

# TRICKS OF STRONG MEN.

:ricks in all trades. The various strong men who are exhibit.
: miraculous strength are not above using a little deception to
or to give more *eclat* to their presentation. A short time
rpreneur wrote to the English paper *Tit Bits* as follows :

ad the pleasure of conducting three of the most celebrated of them
the United States, their feats, genuine and otherwise (the "otherwise"
ates), are of course, perfectly known to me ; as well as the utmost limit to
ach. Indeed, I may say that the utmost capacities of all the strong men
lave been before the public during the last two years are well known to
n this article will be divided into two classes—lifting, and chain, wire,

weight, to be fairly lifted, must be raised until it is at arm's length
ly in an upright position, and must not be allowed to rest on any part
after it has once started thence. The greatest authentic lift ever
y Eugene Sandow at St. James's Hall about September. 1890.
the record, yet he professed nightly at Cardiff, Liverpool, and other
lb.! To my certain knowledge nobody has, either previously or since,
much as 256lb. except on this one occasion, the weights really lifted
what they are said to be. The smaller ones under 100 lbs., only a few
f about 98lb , 150lb., 125lb , and the 200lb., 250lb., 300lb., and 320lb. being
; is known that some competitor is coming upon the stage, when the
a limit of the performer.
iption to the above reductions, that of a dumb-bell belonging to a
w in the States, which weighs 219 lb. 8 oz. without any shot whatever in
hat the balls at the end of all the larger bells are hollow, and fitted with
ley may be loaded with shot or sand at the pleasure of the performer.
is needless to name, but who is now fulfilling an oakum-picking contract
ent, used nightly to lift out of its trolley and carry about the stage a
laimed weighed 1,000lb., and used likewise to offer £50 to any two men
; out of the trolley. This challenge was accepted one night by two
their surprise, as well as that of the spectators, lifted the dumb-bell,
d. The trolley was loaded, and the dumb-bell fixed into it by a catch
r giving the shaft a half turn forward, pushing it along the groove of the
id then turning it back. When this was done, almost anyone could have
ied 78lb.! It is interesting to note that if the balls of this dumb-bell were
to be (they were about 2ft. 6in. in diameter), the whole would weigh

arm's length is done by letting it lie along the fore-arm, this position
eming harder to the uninitiated, whereas it is about 50 per cent easier.
aderful, the lifting from the ground by one of two well-known brothers
as follows. A scaffolding has to be erected over the platform upon which
it the top of this scaffolding, out of sight of the " house." as it moves
ches only, is a lever of the second class, which has its fulcrum on the
f which the strain is reduced by about 50 per cent.
and wire round the chest are merely tricks, and could be done by most
uckle in the first place is filed into an edge, which cuts the leather and
r continued across, soon breaks the strap. In the second case a kink is
as the effect of rotting the metal so to speak at the twist; a wire being
retch, because the expansion of the chest being limited to a few inches,
a if it were to stretch more than that.
king are of two kinds—those which are put over a hook in the stage and
id those that are burst on the biceps or chest. The former, technically
roken by sheer strength, the material of which the links are made being
course unbends as the strain is put on, and is thus stretched apart. The
simple, and are made of hard unstretchable steel, having one breaking
repared for the purpose in several ways, two or three of which it might
on here.
ak with wax, scratching a thin line round one part of it with a needle, and
orie acid or aqua regia, letting the acid corrode the metal until only a
this it must be well washed in water, and then the fine line where the
ks the rest of the chain, which of course conceals the mark effectually.
as there is considerable danger of the fraud being discovered by some
audience who might, on its being handed round for inspection, pull on
the very fact of the chain being painted looks queer.
y better, as it does away with the painting, but far from perfect, is to
en to solder it up again This, however, has the disadvantage of looking
is being examined by the " house."

The method, however, mostly used at present, and seemingly perfect, is to temper the link des hard, so hard in fact that it would break like glass if dropped on a stone slab. Now this link, t break, must have a bending, not a vertical, strain on it, and so must be brought over the sms projection of the biceps, or, in the case of the chest, over the augle of one of the pectorals. As tl right link is only known to the performer, he is safe, as any other man might try for a month an never get the right position.

It might be remarked here that the bicep of the gentleman above referred to as being pro te in Her Majesty's service, was got into that peculiar ball shape by, so to speak, training the muscl by constantly rubbing and pressing it upwards with the hand. This formation is undoubtedly great use in chain-breaking, as it increases the expanding power of the muscle to a very great exter

There is a feat—that of breaking a penny or a shilling—that would be, if it were genuine, whk it is not, the greatest and most wonderful part of all the business of the strong man. This is don in the case of pennies, by placing the coin in a vise and with a pair of pincers, bending it backwar and forwards and until it is soft; the jaws of both instruments being covered with leather so as n to mark the coin. A shilling may be prepared in this way, but it is generally done by covering wi wax, scraping a narrow channel in the same, and putting mercury upon it, which our chemical reade will know, rots the silver so that a breath would almost break it. The wax is then wiped off al the coin rubbed up with a bit of leather, when it looks perfectly natural, as also does the fracture.

The agent or spokesman for the strong man, being fully supplied with pennies or shillings of t most common dates, asks one of the spectators to throw up a penny or a shilling after he has mark it so that he may know it again. As often as not the thrower simply looks at the date, when, course, it is plain sailing for the agent. who has only to be slightly acquainted with palming substitute a prepared coin of the right date. If however, the coin is marked, he gives a prepar one to his man, and when it is broken, throws the pieces over the house, taking care that they not go anywhere near to the person who sent up the original marked coin. It is seldom that t man so treated objects; but. if he does, the agent apoligizes for his mistake, and offers to gi another coin This always ends it, or has at least in my experience, which is not small, for a man not fond of making himself too prominent as a rule. especially in a music-hall.

It is hardly necessary to say that it is not possible to break a coin in the fingers, as, in the fi place, there is hardly anything to take hold of, and in the second, the metal is very hard and toug much harder than one would be led to expect.

Of course, in this business a great deal depends on the *savoir faire* of the agent or spokesma whose patter is 50 per cent. bluff, about 45 per cent. absolute lying, and the rest truth."

## CHAPTER XX.

### THE CONE OF FLOWERS.

In prestigiation flowers have in all times played an important part, and they are usually employed in preference to other objects, since they give the experiments a pleasing aspect. But, in most cases, natural flowers, especially when it is necessary to conceal their presence, are replaced by paper or feather ones, the bulk of which is more easily reduced. Such is the case in the experiment which we are about to present, and which it must be confessed requires to be seen from some little distance in order that the spectators may, without too great an effort of the imagination, be led into the delusion that they are looking at genuine flowers. However, even seen close by, our trick surprises one to the same degree as all those that consist in causing the appearance of more or less bulky objects where nothing was perceived a few moments previously. The prestigiator takes a newspaper and forms it into a cone before one's eyes. It is impossible to suppose the existence here of a double bottom, and yet the cone, gently shaken, becomes filled with flowers that have come from no one knows where. The number of them even becomes so great that they soon more than fill the cone and drop on and cover the floor. The two sides of the flowers employed are represented in Fig. 2, where they are lettered A and B. Each flower consists of four petals of various colors, cut with a punch out of very thin tissue paper. Upon examining Fig. A we see opposite us the petals 1 and 2 and 3 and 4 gummed together by the extremities of their anterior sides, while Fig. B shows us the petals 2 and 3 united in the same manner on the opposite side. A small, very light and thin steel spring (D)

formed of two strips soldered together at the bottom, and pointing in opposite directions, is fixed to the two exterior petals (1 and 4) of the flower, and is concealed by a band of paper of the same color gummed above. It is this spring that, when it is capable of expanding freely, opens the flower and gives it its voluminous aspect. Quite a large number of these flowers (a hundred or more), united, and held together by means of a thread or a rubber band (Fig. 2, C), makes a package small enough to allow the operator to conceal it in the palm of his hand, only the back of which he allows the spectators to see while he is forming the paper cone.

## CHANGING INK INTO WATER.

The trick consists in placing on a table a glass half-full of ink. The audience is shown a white card, which is dipped into the liquid and taken out stained black. A handkerchief is thrown over the glass, lifted up again, when pure water is found in the place of ink. It is done in this way: Place inside against the glass a strip of black silk of the same height as the level of the water, which will then appear, from

a distance, to be ink. Take a card, part of which you have stained black on one side only. Show the unstained side to the audience before dipping, and when taking it out again turn it round so as to show the black part. You now throw a handkerchief over the glass and seize hold of the piece of cloth inside the glass, removing it inside the handkerchief; the water will then assume its ordinary appearance.

## FIRE DRAWINGS.

If a very strong or saturated solution of saltpetre be used with a quill or fine brush to make a drawing or writing on thin white absorbent paper (the lines being kept well clear of each other, and the whole in outline), when quite dry the end of a glowing match without flame will set fire to the lines, and a spark will run along the design, cutting it out as with a knife. The saltpetre yields oxygen to combine with the carbon of the paper, when heated to the point of ignition by the glowing charcoal of a match ignited and blown out.

## CHAPTER XXI.

## TRICKS WITH LIONS AND WILD BEASTS.

LION HUNTER.

Some years ago a very interesting article appeared in the *New York Sun* upon the training and handling of wild beasts in general and lions in particular, and so much does this article coincide with my own opinion, gleaned from much observation and close questioning of animal trainers and workers, that I venture to insert a considerable portion of the writer's remarks :

"As a matter of fact," said John B. Doris, the well-known museum manager, but formerly a circus proprietor of some thirty years' experience, "there is no animal with which we circus men have to deal that is so easy to handle and so safe for a performer as a lion. In everything they are just like great big good-natured dogs, easy to train and more than ordinarily easy to perform. In fact, after they are once trained to do their tricks, anybody with whom they are acquainted, such as an attendant or a man whom they have been accustomed to see around the show, can go into their cage and put them through their act with perfect safety. Why, in one season I had no less than eleven men perform my lions, and in each case these men were feeders, canvas-men, hostlers and other employees of the circus who would be apt to be about the animals all the time."

### ROARS BECAUSE HAPPY.

"It is the appearance of the lion and that dreadful roar of his that strikes terror into the heart of the spectator and causes him to think that he is in great danger; but that roar of the lion, while so dreadful in sound, is like a good many other things in the show business, more of a deception than otherwise. A lion really only roars when he is in a particularly good humor, and he can no more help doing it than can a dog help barking."

"An incident occurred with my show in Indianapolis which proves how great the terror a lion will cause and how really docile he is. We were fixing up in the spring of 1886 to go on the road in the Exposition building, and I believe there were three hundred men at work in the building. One of my men, named Pearl Sowder, was transferring the four lions from the old cage to the newly painted wagon, when, by the carelessness of one of the attendants, the door flew open and two of the animals, Romeo and George, jumped out and started across the room towards a couple of barrels that contained fat from the meat with which the animals were fed. The minute they struck the ground somebody spied them and shouted, ' The lions are loose ! ' In a half minute—yes, in less time than that—every one of those three hundred men was out of that building, and they didn't stop for doors, either ; they went through windows, taking sash, glass and everything else.''

''Sowders heard the noise, and looking round, jumped out of the cage, ran across the room, grabbed Romeo by the scruff of the neck and dragged him back and literally booted him into the cage, and then served George the same way. All those two lions cared for was the fat in the barrel. I paid $80 for the glass, though, that the men broke when they went through the windows, and so my recollection of that incident is a vivid one.''

## SUSCEPTIBLE OF MUCH TRAINING.

The two animals Mr. Doris spoke of as jumping out of the cage were two of the best-trained animals ever shown in America, and when Doris sold out his circus the Orrin Brothers bought them and took them down to Mexico, where they are still performing. Romeo was afterwards trained by a man named Volta to do the riding act, and it is said that the exhibition of the lions in a bull pen in Vera Cruz by the Orrins netted them $10,000 in one week. This part of Romeo's act consisted of crouching on a padded horse while the horse was galloping around the ring, and then, at the word of command, jumping over a banner and alighting on the pad again. Romeo has also been taught to walk a narrow plank, much in the same fashion as a tight rope.

Prof. George Conkling, who is Barnum & Bailey's animal trainer, smiled when asked if lions were dangerous, and said :

'' Well, no ; I should think not. And there are only two animals that we have anything to do with that are dangerous ; one is an elephant and the other a leopard. Lions are very easily broken and very easily performed after being broken. Why, I took four lions when the Barnum show went into winter quarters and broke them to do a half-dozen tricks in two weeks, in addition to training dens of wolves, bears, hyenas, leopards, tigers and pumas. The way I usually train animals is to give them an hour to two hours' practise morning and afternoon. In training lions, we begin with the simplest of tricks ; for instance, take the act of a lion jumping through a hoop. One attendant holds the hoop on the ground and the lion is made to walk through ; if he does not walk through or does not understand, why take hold of the back of his neck and haul him through. After he knows that he has got to go through that hoop anyway, it is lifted up a little higher from the ground, until finally the desired height is reached.''

## ''VERY EASILY DONE—TRY IT.''

'' How do you train a lion so that you can get your head in his mouth ? ''

'' That doesn't require any training ; just yank his mouth open and put your head in.''

'' How about the sensation when the lion stands up and puts his paws on your shoulders ? ''

'' Well, we lift him up until he is made to understand that he must get up himself. The usual performances of the lions are in this manner : The cage is divided into three compartments, with a door between each, and the trainer goes in there and he first makes a picture ; he stands in the centre with a whip in his hand, while one lion stands up with his paws on the cage in one corner, and then crouches in one end, and the other two squat and watch him in a restless fashion ; and then the trainer puts them through all their tricks, separately and together, such as jumping over a pole and through a hoop bound with oakum and saturated with naptha, all flaming ; puts his head in their mouths, and winds up the act by firing rapidly a six-barrelled revolver, and jumps out and slams the door of the cage behind him. And if he has an especially well-trained lion, as he slams the gate that lion will jump against the bars and make them rattle."

"How are they trained to jump against the bars?"

"In the same way they are trained to jump over a pole. We wind up the act in the same way every night, and the closing of the gate is a signal for the lion to jump."

## KINDNESS AND RAWHIDE.

"Are they amenable to kindness, Mr. Conkling?"

"Yes; but they are much more amenable to the discipline of the gad. But they are unlike other animals in this particular: they do not have to be constantly watched after once broken. A leopard is treacherous, and no matter whether you have worked him ten years or ten days, if you take your eye off of him for one instant he will strike you. Of course, some animals are more easily trained than others, and so when we get a lion that is not easily broken we don't waste time on him, but set him aside and train those that are most intelligent."

"Are there many performing lions in the United States?"

"Well, I couldn't say just how many, but there are a great number. Mr. Forepaugh had so many at one time, over thirty, that he gave them away for almost nothing to save the cost of his meat bill. They breed very easily and the female is prolific; she will have a litter every six months of three to five cubs, and, as the whelps are ordinarily healthy, and breeding of lions has been going on for the past thirty years, there must be a great many throughout the United States. A good specimen, full grown and well broken male is worth $2,000."

One of the animal attendants at Central Park had something to say about lions, and he confirmed the statements of Mr. Doris and Mr. Conkling as to their docile qualities. He said:

"Young man, have you ever seen an attendant clean out a cage? He just gets in there and sweeps away, and if the big 'cat' is in the way, he sweeps him to one side with the dirt; there is no more harm in lions to a man that knows 'em than there is in a big dog. I'll tell you a curious thing about lions and animals. Just watch animals that are fat and healthy, and then you look at the man that takes care of them and feeds them, and you'll find that he is a great, big red-faced healthy man himself. Animals don't like thin, consumptive-looking chaps, and they get thin and worry and lose their tempers with that kind of attendants. I was with Forepaugh for ten years, and he wouldn't have a thin man 'round the show—that is, near the animals. No, I never did hear of a man being bitten or scratched by a lion except one man, and he didn't know his business. Why, lion performances are so common that the circus people don't think the act any good any more, and a lion trainer can't get over $30 a month. That's the reason I quit the circus business. I can remember a time when there was good money in it. I first went with Van Amburgh, who was the greatest animal trainer that ever lived."

## TIGER CATCHING IN THE DARK.

Every season, while a circus is traveling around the country, wrecks occur. Cages get smashed and animals get out. When that is the case, and a lion gets out of the cage which is his home, he doesn't know what to do, and crouches on the ground, much more frightened than the people around him, and he stays there until somebody takes and puts him in his cage or brings the cage up to him, and then he will jump in. A good illustrative instance of that kind occurred in a railroad accident in a tunnel just outside of Baltimore about two years ago. In the

Cole show the lion and tiger cages were wrecked in the centre of the tunnel, and the lion got out and roamed through the tunnel in the dark, until finally he .walked out at one end and jumped into an empty cage. But Mr. Cole had to take a lantern and go in the tunnel and secure the black tiger himself, which he did without much difficulty.

There is a school for the training of animals, or properly a building in which animals are trained, on the edge of the meadows at the back of Jersey City Heights, and over there is a lion whelp being trained to do some remarkable tricks. Already he can see-saw on a board, stand up on his hind paws and walk a few feet, drag a wagon around while harnessed to it, and his trainer is trying to make him wind up his performance by trotting off to his cage carrying the apparently senseless body of his master in his mouth. If he succeeds in thoroughly training him, and it looks now as if he would, the lion will undoubtedly be worth a mint to Mr. Seaman, his master.

INDIAN SNAKE CHARMERS.

## CHAPTER XXII.

### WHAT THE PAPERS SAY.

Speaking about Professor Baldwin a writer in the Leeds (Eng.) *Express* says :—

"Sometimes the spirits will work ; sometimes they won't."

We have Professor Baldwin's word for it. They worked on me the other day and lured me up to the Professor's diggings, where I spent half an hour in discussing with him his big show and "how it's done." It was not likely that he would voluntarily unbosom himself as to the means by which he presents such a marvelous performance. But there was the off-chance that the Professor, who is pensive and guileless, might let slip a thing or two that would blow the gaff, as Charles Reade used to say. I was lucky beyond expectation. There is nothing like concealment about Mr. Baldwin. He is open as the day ; and answered with artless cordiality all my questions. His candor is delightful ; and as public curiosity has been excited by the Baldwins' Coliseum performances as nothing has excited them within recollections, I mean to let my readers into all the secrets I gleaned in the half hour I spent with Mr. and Mrs. Baldwin.

I say " the half hour spent " because that is the limit I mentally fixed upon when I yielded to the spirit impulse. As a matter of fact, that half hour stretched out to three hours or more ; and I suspect I should have been there still had not the arrival of their carriage to take them to the Coliseum warned me that I was keeping Mr. and Mrs. Baldwin from their audience.

The fact is, the fascination attaching to their performance attaches also to themselves—which cannot always be said of entertainers. You forget all about the flight of time, as you discuss theories and manifestations and suggestions with the talented couple, or enjoy an "intermission" in which Mrs. Baldwin—a brilliant and vivacious conversationalist—tells you of her visit to the Mikado, and the magnificent dresses and jewels he presented her with, or Mr. Baldwin interests you with an account of Salt Lake City and Brigham Young, of the beheading of Chinese pirates in Hong Kong, or of his experiences among the Mahatmas of Thibet, the diamond-mining camps of South Africa, the temples of Japan, the palaces of Indian Rajahs, in the groves of Burmah, or the mining villages of Nevada. You may readily imagine, therefore, that the three hours sped away with a greased lightning-like rapidity which I did not anticipate when I knocked at the door.

" Come in ! Don't be afraid of the spirits ! "

That was the Professor's salutation.

I might have told him that the spirits were not yet distilled, let alone bottled, before which any man would quail. But I didn't. I merely said—

"Chestnut ! I heard you say that in your entertainment."

The Professor did not attempt to deny it.

" Come right in, then," said he, "and let me tell you something you have not heard from me before."

I came in—" right in," as the Professor cordially expressed it ; and he amply redeemed his promise. In their friendly presence I even forgot my trepidation as to whether Mrs. Baldwin—who can pinck the unwritten thought from the mind, to say nothing of the unseen written question from the waistcoat pocket—would not read within my breast the unconfessed designs I harbored upon the secrets of their show. Perhaps she did, for all I know. But she was as delightfully agreeable as strawberries and cream on a scorching August day.

I tackled the Professor first upon his Cabinet trick. I thought it politic here to trust to his magnanimity. So I simply confessed that I could not understand how, while tied hard and fast, he contrives to loose his hand, to slip a tambourine over the head of the very committeeman who is examining his bonds, and yet to replace his hand before the committeeman can detect him.

"And £100 for a loose knot," observed the Professor, sententiously. "But they never find it."

" Do you never expect someone who has watched your performance previously, and knows the points, to come on prepared to detect you just as you have freed yourself ?"

The Professor smiled.

" It has been tried scores of times," said he, "but the result is just the same. The inquisitor finds the tambourine around his neck just when he least expects it, and my hand firmly fastened again."

" You are not a believer in spiritualism ?"

" Not in the least !" This very emphatically. " On the contrary, I have devoted considerable time to confounding the pretentions of spiritualists and exposing their manifestations, particularly in America. I have attended scores of their seances, unknown and unsuspected ; and I have never seen a manifestation which I was not able to reproduce a few days afterwards."

" Then your allusions to the spirits must be taken as sly fun ?"

" I claim no occult or supernatural powers. I produce my effects by purely natural means." "By the way, you have performed a good deal in the East, Professor. Is not Western magic somewhat at a discount in that region of the mystic and fantastic ?"

" Quite the reverse," was the reply. " We go into the very home of mystery and magic, and beat them on their own ground. The stories of Indian jugglery are much exaggerated ; and their performances fall far below ours. We draw great audiences in India, and the Rajahs and Maharajahs, before whom all the best native mystery men appear, are delighted and amazed with our entertainment."

And then the Professor brings out a huge scrapbook crammed with photographs of Indian potentates and palaces before and in which their performances have been given ; and supplements this with the production of caskets and boxes containing a profusion of costly gems, jewels, &c.—the presents of these appreciative Native Princes.

" But the Mahatmas, Professor—you spent some time amongst them investigating their mysteries ?"

" Yes ; but I found their claims to be untenable. All the manifestations the Mahatmas produce I can obtain by natural means, and that is how they obtain them—their claims to the contrary notwithstanding. And very clumsy some of their methods are. Did you ever see a Mahatma, by the way ?" And the Professor opened the big scrapbook at another page. Here are photographs of a group of them. The upper lot, you will notice, wear great grotesque and ugly masks over their heads. Below, you see them with the masks removed."

Mahatmas went down in my estimation with that revelation. The masks are startling from their hideousness ; the faces are not striking, either for excessive ugliness to great intelligence.

" Now, as to the Somnomancy, Professor. There are many people—generally, I admit, those who have not seen it—who assert that it is a mere pretence. Is that so ?"

The Professor became grave.

" It is no use trying to convince some people. They think disbelief shown cleverness. Now, I tell you, I have the most perfect belief in it ; and my confidence in my wife's work is unshakable."

" Is Mrs. Baldwin, when she comes out of the hypnotic state, conscious of the replies she has given, or the questions she has answered ?"

" Not in the least. She is a mere irresponsible agent. She forms a mind picture of the matter upon which a question is asked, and so supplies the answer ; but she knows no more about it. I never claim that all her answers are correct ; but about 80 or 85 per cent. are."

" What puzzles me is how she obtains the question in order to form the mental picture that answers it ?"

- "Mrs. Baldwin is the possessor of gifts that belong to extremely few organizations. The test of the genuineness of the replies is the fact that every night nearly a hundred questions are answered which have been written down or merely thought of by people who are utter strangers, and who are yet told facts concerning the past of themselves or their friends which are admittedly correct. It is fair to assume, then, that what is foretold for the future is equally correct."

Then we fell into abtruse and recondite discussion, which, I fear, would be of little interest to the reader, but in which the earnestness and virile mental power of the man were convincingly shown. And so, with more displays of precious stones—rubies from Burmah, rose diamonds, green rubies, sparkling amethysts, gold chains of Indian make—and photographs in many lands, and of other valued possessions, my interview sped on to its close, when I came away resolved to tell you all the mysteries I have unravelled.

### A writer in the Hartford (Conn.) *Post* says :—

The sensation of the week has been the wonderful entertainment of the Baldwins given every evening at Foot Guard Hall. Its marvellous and fascinating excellence was best shown by the increasing size of the audiences from night to night. Last evening the big armory was crowded. The unique feature that closed the entertainment each evening—"somnomancy," it is called on the programme—"clairvoyance," or "mind-reading" as others term it—has fairly astounded the public. It has been the town topic. Barbers have stopped discussing pugilistic events to debate the nature of Mrs. Baldwin's strange power. The exhibition has been the food of exciting parlor talks in many homes, it has been the text of nine out of ten of the groups seen on the street corners, and it has held its own against political subjects, which is saying a great deal in these exciting pre-election times. Briefly expressed, Mrs. Baldwin by answering questions written on paper that never goes into her possession, offers a mystery that baffles the best.

The personality of people who can make such a furore in the community cannot but be interesting.

Everybody wants to know about Mrs. Baldwin. She is a young English woman of trim figure and a face pretty in its brightness. It reflects the possession of the highest order of intelligence combined with a merry heart that sends a constant smile to the surface. She speaks with a slight English accent. Until she came to this country a few months ago, she had been everywhere but America, so that she does not feel so strange among the customs here, having had the experience of being a "foreigner" many times before. She likes America very well.

One thing about Mrs. Baldwin that will interest the ladies is, that she makes her own dresses. She has a special talent in that line, some of her creations being worthy of a Worth, without an attempt at a pun. She gets an idea for a dress, for the stage or the street, and in whatever town she happens to be she sends out for a couple of expert seamstresses, and when the job is done she has more cause for satisfaction than the ordinary woman with a new gown. The fact is, she is a very versatile little lady. Besides her grand, mystifying "somnomancy," she can give enough specialties to make an entire evening's entertainment, if it were not too fatiguing.

Her clever work, in which she impersonates various characters and sings appropriately to each, is decidedly unique.

Her automatic dancer, little Nick Russell, is another idea of her own that always takes well. It must be seen to have the real ingenuity and fun of the thing appreciated. Then she does a monologue introducing bright lines, taking songs well rendered, and some very graceful dancing. She seems to be able to do all her specialties equally well. It is common for a person to be able to do a little of everything and nothing very well of anything. But not so with Mrs. Baldwin. She is as happy and successful in each of her forms of entertaining as she is puzzling and theory-defying in what must be called her chief talent. That she has been received with great cordiality wherever she has appeared in this country is a triumph to be proud of, for many of her kind come across and few are chosen.

The life of Professor Baldwin and Mrs. Baldwin *en tour* is a busy one. An extra room is always engaged by them to be used as an office. I dropped in at the "office" yesterday morning and found the place to look "for all the world" like the local headquarters of a party during a political campaign. Several tables were piled high with papers, letters, circulars and envelopes. The floor was carpeted with similar material, and the heads of two secretaries digging into the heap could just be seen over the top. Both secretaries are stenographers, and are needed to assist in attending to the enormous correspondence that comes in like small avalanches. No callers are received. Professor Baldwin is kept hustling pretty much all day long superintending the work.

I found "The White Mahatma," as Professor Baldwin is called on account of his acquaintance with the Indian mysteries, inclined to take a rest from some work he was at, and he kindly offered to send to the bank for his collection of jewels so that I might see them. I was only too delighted at the opportunity, and on the messenger returning I had the pleasure of a rare treat in the valuables displayed.

Most of the jewels he showed me are dear to him from some association, being gifts from admirers in India and elsewhere. Chief among the treasures, not for its intrinsic worth but in interest, is a curious gold watch, a gift from the Maharajah of Pattialia. It is of French make, very old and in the centre of the dial are two figures who strike the hours and quarters with hammers upon miniature bells. The watch has a history, being originally given by an English King to a favorite, and in the course of human events coming into the possession of a British officer who was killed in the India mutiny. The old Rajah of Pattialla got the watch and left it to his son, the Rajah who presented it to Professor Baldwin. Other souvenirs of great value are a tortoise-shell snuff-box bearing upon its lid under crystal a perfect view of a boar hunt in carved gold, the gift of the Maharajah of Gwalior; a great opal surrounded by diamonds, given to Mrs. Baldwin by the Sultan of Johore; a gold chain, heavy and seven feet long, given to Mrs. Baldwin by another eastern potentate; a fine specimen of gold fret work on a background of emerald enamel; a gold cross set with diamonds from the Prince of Wales, and a lot of other costly trinkets.

Then the loose stones! There were boxes and boxes of them, of all sorts and conditions. His rubies are especially fine.

He showed me two of the rarest stones in the world—rose-colored diamonds set in rings, worth several thousands of dollars each.

He has other jewel freaks, like white sapphires, green diamonds, green rubies, rubies with a little of the red and the green blended into each, and a dozen other odd varieties; I can't begin to do the exhibition justice now, for I wasted all my superlatives at the time. Better than all was to watch the Professor in his element. He picked out of a box of a hundred or more rubies, with his tweezers, this or that stone that was a little better than its neighbors, that had a richer wine color, or that was of a peculiar shape, blaming the cloudy weather all the time because it would not allow the setting forth of his pets at their best. So much for Professor Baldwin's hobby. Now for himself. After paralyzing me with the splendor of his gems, Professor Baldwin brought me back to life with the remark that he was once a reporter. I had been in a trance like unto Mrs. Baldwin's, and was trying to give myself an answer that some day I would be very wealthy and give up collecting stamps for rubies, when the Professor made his abrupt remark. Of course it made me the more sanguine.

"I was born in Cincinnati," the Mahatma said, "and had a whack at studying theology and medicine, but gave up both and enlisted, and after the war was a reporter on a paper. In the course of my work I attended a so-called spiritualistic seance, and my interest in the mysterious has been maintained ever since. I have made the circle of the globe four times. Twice I have retired with a fortune, but this is a fascinating business to me. I am made for it, and I expect to die as I have lived so long—before the public."